LOVE ME ***by Bella Andre***

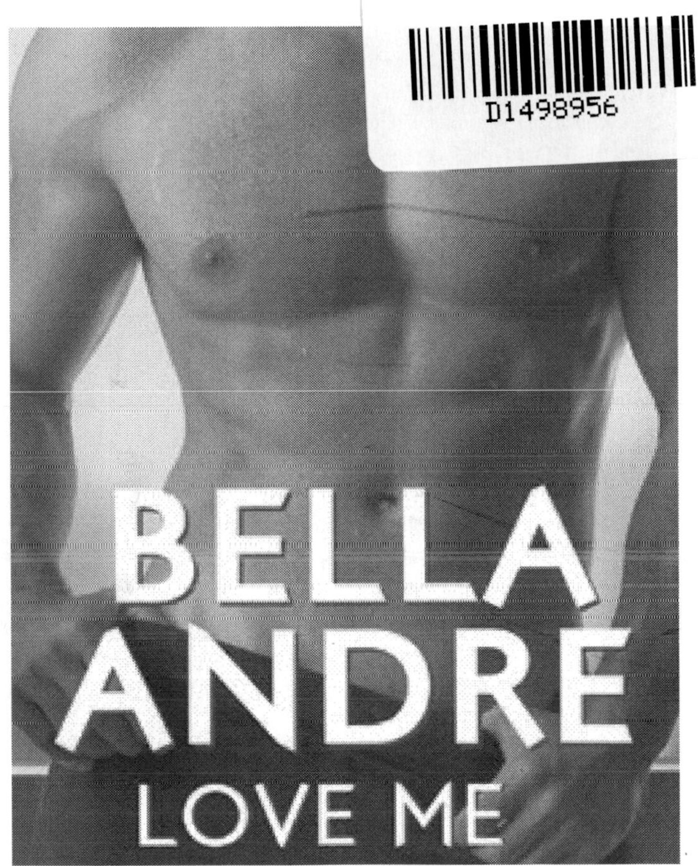

Love Me
(Take Me sequel)

Chapter One

"Car accident. Ten-year-old girl. Possible ruptured spleen."

Luke Carson dropped the x-ray he was groggily reviewing to run beside the frightened girl who was rapidly losing blood. Her cheeks were stained with tear tracks and her long blond hair blew off the side of the gurney as the nurses wheeled her into surgery. She looked up at Luke with big, barely conscious blue eyes.

"I know you don't feel so good right now, honey, but in a few seconds everything will be better. I'm going to take care of you."

"Promise?" she whispered.

"I promise." He would do everything in his power not to let her, or her family, down.

He held out his hands for surgical gloves just as Robert, another trauma surgeon who'd come on an hour earlier, popped his head in the door.

"You've been on for twenty-four, Luke. You

want me to take this one for you?"

"Nope. I've got it."

Saving lives was not just a job for Luke. Being a trauma surgeon was what he'd been born to do. He was the best man for the job. It wasn't arrogance.

It was the truth.

Luke was ten years old when he decided to become a doctor. Even though the rest of his friends – and his brother, Travis - had been out partying in their twenties, he didn't regret a single one of the long hours he'd spent in class or poring over thick textbooks in the library. His number one priority had always been to save lives. Because he knew what happened to families when somebody died.

They fell apart.

Every parent he brought back from the brink meant there was one more kid who had a dad to play ball with and a mom to kiss him goodnight. And every child he took care of meant there was one less devastated parent trying to pick up the pieces of their life.

Luke's job was everything to him. Especially on nights like this when a little girl's life was at stake.

He had caught a very brief flash of her parent's faces as they ran into the ER behind the paramedics. They'd been scared, more frightened than they'd ever been before. If she died, the hole in their hearts would never be healed

Luke couldn't let that happen. But when he moved to press the scalpel down onto the girl's skin, he suddenly realized he couldn't control his hands.

Shit.

He pulled his hands away and took a deep breath. Surgery required complete concentration. His strength of will had never failed him before. But even with his hands still at his sides, he could feel the shaking grow worse, damn it.

He looked up and was surprised to see Robert standing unobtrusively against the wall, looking concerned, but waiting for Luke's cue. When had his colleague come into the OR? Had it been that obvious to him that Luke wasn't up to the job tonight?

Fuck, no. He could do it. He was going to stand by his promise to save the little girl's life.

A second later, everything began to blur, and he felt Robert's hand on his arm, steadying him.

"I'm fresh, Luke. Let me take this."

Luke had to fight like hell not to shake off Robert's hand.

Damn it. He'd worked plenty of twenty-four-hour shifts. He should be able to pull this off.

Only, this was about a hell of a lot more than "pulling it off." This was life and death for an innocent ten-year-old girl. Every second counted in the ER. He'd already wasted too many.

If the girl died it would be his fault. He'd have to face her parents and tell them that his ego had killed her. And he'd never forgive himself.

"Robert," his said in a low voice, "go ahead and take over."

His friend quickly stepped in, taking not

only the instruments from Luke, but his control over the situation as well.

For the first time in years, Luke didn't know what to do. The only thing that was clear was that he was no longer needed. Robert and the nursing staff had everything well under control.

They'd save the girl. They had to.

All he knew for sure was that if he'd stayed, if he hadn't stepped away and finally handed over the reins, his hands might have slipped at a crucial moment.

He could have killed her.

On leaden feet he left the OR, walked down the hallway, and entered the locker room. He ripped off his scrubs and threw them toward the overflowing hamper in the cluttered locker room at San Francisco General Hospital. No surprise, the bundle of blood-laced green fabric missed the basket. By a mile.

He should have gone home twelve hours ago. But he hadn't. Because he had nothing—*no one*—to go home to.

He dragged his hands over his face, through too-long dark hair that was just beginning to curl at the base of his neck. Standing in front of the scratched and dirty mirror in the corner of the locker room, his bloodshot eyes stared back at him accusingly.

He'd been on the verge of overstepping his bounds as a doctor.

Because he'd thought he could play God instead.

LOVE ME *by Bella Andre*

Luke wanted to tell himself that what had happened tonight was a fluke, a one-time deal. That he was in control of his life.

In the past few years he'd pushed himself harder. Worked longer hours. Saved more lives. Sewed up more chests. Pulled out more bullets.

But for some reason, they were empty victories. And, lately, he'd been thinking more and more about why that was, if it had something to do with coming home to an empty house. No wife. No kids.

So far, however, he hadn't met anyone he could imagine wanting around forever.

His last girlfriend was a business analyst who worked nearly as many hours as he did. She'd been attractive, but cold, and even though she'd always warmed up in bed, he hadn't been able to shake the feeling that they just weren't a good fit. Even though she should have been perfect for him. Before Laura, there'd been Christine. Another bright, attractive, mature woman. A prominent economist, she also wrote regularly for the Chronicle. But she hadn't cared for his hours and when she'd given him an ultimatum - her or his job - the choice had been easy. Goodbye Christine.

The truth was, when he looked back, all of his ex-girlfriends blurred together. Attractive. Driven. Mature. Sensible.

Boring.

He stripped off his boxers and white T-shirt and stepped beneath the hot spray in the shower stall, barely feeling the water pelt him across the chest as he quickly shampooed and soaped up. He felt broken, used up. Miles beyond exhausted.

He shut the water off and shook like a dog in the small laminate cubicle. He wrapped a towel around his waist and stepped out of the shower.

Elizabeth, a new resident, said, "Hello, Luke," to let him know he was no longer alone in the room. She was exactly the kind of woman he'd usually ask out. A cool, reserved blonde, she turned away quickly so that he could have his privacy getting dressed.

For a moment, Luke thought about it. He wasn't seeing anyone right now, and it had been too long since he'd gotten release outside of his hand in the shower.

But he discarded the idea as quickly as it came. Judging by the way his cock was just laying there utterly limp beneath the towel, trying to act like he was into her would be a hell of a lot more work than it was worth.

Not to mention the fact that he didn't do one-night stands. Never had. He'd left that territory to Travis, who'd settled down with Luke's best friend, Lily, five years ago. They'd married in a surprise ceremony in Tuscany and had two great kids.

Luke was happy for them—of course he was—and yet, their perfect relationship only seemed to highlight everything he was missing. Thinking of his brother and sister-in-law and their happiness only made the thought of going home with a virtual stranger more distasteful.

"Elizabeth," he said with a curt nod, reaching for the clean jeans and shirt in his locker and quickly dressing. Taking the stairs down to the underground parking garage, he got in behind the wheel of his Porsche and turned the key in the ignition. Pulling out onto the empty, dark street he was about to turn right, up the hill to his house in Pacific Heights. But he couldn't face his big empty house tonight. And he couldn't barge in on Lily and Travis. Not at 1:30 a.m. when the whole family was already asleep.

On a night like this, where everything he thought to be true, to be real, had spiraled out of control, there was only one thing left that might help him hold on to the remains of his sanity: the one woman he couldn't have.

And the only one he'd ever wanted.

Instead of going right, he turned left, heading for South of Market.

Heading straight to Janica.

LOVE ME *by Bella Andre*

Chapter Two

"Hey baby, Nick and I are seriously into this."

Janica Ellis looked up from uncapping a couple of beers for her two guests and forced a smile at Jarod.

A half hour ago she'd gone by one of her regular haunts and picked up not just one guy, but two. She was just so fucking bored.

Of course she was thrilled with the success of her clothing line, J Style. She loved spending time with her sister, Lily, and Lily's kids. And between her girlfriends and the guys she dated, Janica almost never sat home alone in front of the TV on a Saturday night.

Still, even great sex with a hot guy got old after a while. Particularly if it was sex with the wrong hot guy.

The problem was, so far they'd all been the wrong guy. She'd been dating since she was fourteen but she'd never been in love with any of her boyfriends. Not even close.

Maybe, she'd started to think, some people were hardwired to fall in love – like Lily who had fallen head-over-heels in love with Travis as kids -

and some people weren't.

In any case, even if Janica was missing the love gene, she still needed to figure out what to do about tonight.

Lately she'd read a bunch of books with ménages. They seemed pretty kinky. Exciting. And for a second, when she'd let the guys know what she was up for, and they'd accepted, it had been a rush. But before they'd even made it out of the bar, the thrill had fizzled away.

Right now she didn't feel any more excited about what she was about to do with two hunks than she had about any of her previous lovers for the past year.

Sure, they'd probably make her come in some sort of really inventive three-way position. But so what? She could come just fine on her own.

Good thinking, Janica, she said to herself in a sarcastic voice. *How in hell are you planning to get them to leave now?*

"Hey, I know I suggested this three-way, but guess what? I was just kidding."

Not only were the odds of them laughing damn low, any woman with half a brain could easily guess they weren't going to be too gung ho about leaving either.

Lately, she'd been grading her impulsive actions more and more, having these annoyed, silent conversations. Thankfully, she still felt great about her business, but on every other front—whether she was a good enough sister, a good enough friend, a good enough person, period—she wasn't at all sure.

LOVE ME *by Bella Andre*

For the first twenty-nine years of her life, she hadn't given a second thought to any of those things. She'd simply decided what she wanted and gone after it.

She hadn't wasted time on worry or regret, on trying to "act her age." She'd focused on squeezing every last ounce of joy out of life, on racking up exhilarating life experiences.

But something had changed this past year, as she'd rounded the corner toward thirty. No, not something.

Her.

She had changed. Out of the blue, she suddenly found herself lying in bed thinking about all the things she'd never wanted before. Real love. Someone to come home to at night. Someone to laugh with. Someone to plan with. Someone to share new things with.

Luke.

Damn it. Why couldn't she control her thoughts about him?

Twenty-five years ago it had started as a secret crush, a little girl spying on a big boy with a heart-melting smile. And it had turned into an obsession. A stupid, pathetic obsession that only got worse with every family event she went to.

Five years after Lily had married Luke's twin brother, Travis, Janica was still a little bit shocked by it all. She loved Lily more than anyone else on the planet and, yet, who would have thought that her shy, insecure older sister would have found true love first? Janica had always been the popular one, with all the friends, all the style, and all the confidence. But now Lily had a gorgeous husband who adored her while Janica was so cynical about men and ever falling in love that she'd actually invited two of them into her bed.

Beyond pissed at herself, she walked out from the kitchen with the beers. “Here.”

Instead of taking the bottles, the guys shot each other a look and started pulling their shirts out from their pants. Okay, so having a threesome probably wasn't going to suck, but no matter how she tried to spin it in her head, “not sucking” just wasn't a good enough reason for doing it.

Maybe if she were the heroine in a romance novel it would be okay. But this wasn't fantasy. This was real life.

Her life.

“You know what boys,” she began, “I don't think—”

She was cut off by the doorbell.

What the hell? Who could possibly be coming to see her at 1:30 in the morning?

Oh God, she immediately thought, *something has happened to Lily or the kids.*

Panicked, she flew to the door and yanked it open.

It took her brain longer than it should have to register the fact that Luke Carson was standing in front of her, long enough for him to take her completely unaware with his hands on her shoulders.

And his mouth hard and hot on hers.

In an instant, everything fell away but his kiss. It was hungry, like a trapped lion who'd broken through his chains and could finally unleash the urge to devour his prey whole.

He wasn't asking, he was taking.

Demanding.

A hundred times—no, at least a thousand times—she'd dreamed of kissing Luke, had stared at his mouth, at his lips, and wondered how they'd feel pressed up against her skin. And yet, even her best fantasies, even the ones that had her crying out his name in bed with one of her battery-operated toys, didn't begin to come close to this beautiful reality.

My God, he was delicious. A spicy, darkly sensual aphrodisiac. Powerful and satisfying.

He forced his tongue into her mouth, ruthless as he sucked her breath into his body. She moaned with pleasure that came from way deep down in her core and wrapped her hands around his rock-hard butt to pull him closer.

His hands were rough, unyielding as they curved hard into the small of her back, then tightly gripped the curve of her ass. All space, all air between them was completely obliterated in his full-on assault on her mouth, her body.

"What the hell?"

"Who the fuck is he?"

Two male voices spoke almost in unison.

Oh crap. She'd completely forgotten about her would-be fuck buddies.

Luke yanked his mouth away from hers to look up and over her shoulder. It was, Janica thought, like watching a really messy accident happen in slow motion. You almost felt like you could step in and stop it from happening if you were quick enough. Even though the truth was she didn't have a chance in hell of halting the crash.

Luke growled a succinct, “Get out,” at the two men.

“Wait a minute,” Nick said, stepping forward. “We were here first.”

Luke all but puffed out his chest and bared his teeth. “I said get the fuck out.”

When he acted like this she was almost scared of him. She'd never seen Luke look so menacing. Or so possessive. A delicious little shiver ran through her.

All this time she'd thought she had him completely figured out. She'd been absolutely certain he was a type A, arrogant surgeon, destined for a blond trophy wife to decorate his suburban home and carpool his J. Crew clad kids to soccer games. She'd pegged him as Mr. Perfect, someone who had never uttered a curse word in his life. Amazingly, the word “fuck” sounded just right on his tongue.

If she was wrong about that, then what else was she wrong about?

Janica opened her mouth to tell the boys she was going to send them home anyway and Luke's hands tightened on her shoulders.

“Don't you say a damn word.”

Again, desire rode through her at his command. She'd tried the whole master-submissive thing once—with her as the dominatrix, of course, in a leather corset and "fuck me" boots—but hurting someone to get them off hadn't been her cup of tea.

Luke's tough-guy act, on the other hand, was exactly her brand of Earl Grey.

Unfortunately, the boys she'd met at the bar weren't too quick on the uptake.

"Fuck you, man," Jarod said. "We were here first. We're staying."

Again, Janica tried to say something, but Luke pulled her so hard against him she actually lost her breath.

"She just uninvited you, asshole. Both of you."

The two guys advanced on Luke and that was when she decided enough was enough. No way was she going to waste precious lip-lock time with Luke on what was sure to be a bloody fight with these bozos.

Another time she'd let three guys fight over her. Right now there was only one thing she wanted: to be alone, preferably naked, with the man of her dreams.

"I'm really sorry, guys, but I completely forgot about this appointment I had with Luke."

Their mouths fell open in a particularly unattractive way. How had she ever found their beefy-arms and crew-cuts attractive?

"Appointment? In the middle of the night?"

"Do you think we're stupid enough to believe that?"

Yes, actually she did.

During the short exchange she could feel Luke simmering beside her, but even though his coming in and taking over was a total turn-on, it had also started to piss her off a little bit.

She could take care of herself, thank you, had been doing just that for twenty-nine years. Well, apart from the fact that Lily had pretty much raised her after their parents died, she'd been going it alone her whole life.

Deciding to show all of them that it was her apartment, damn it, and she'd decide who stayed and who left, using every bit of strength in her small body, she wrenched herself out of Luke's vise hold, picked up the guys' jackets and carried them over to the open door.

"Sorry this didn't work out."

Clearly furious, they stomped across the room and yanked their jackets from her.

"Cock tease."

Before she even realized he'd moved, Luke had Nick's shirt in his fists.

"Don't you ever talk to a woman like that again." Each word held a world of menace. "Apologize to her, asshole." He waited a beat and when nothing came, he said, "Right fucking now."

Nick's face was beet red and Janica wasn't at all sure that he could breathe.

"Sorry," he squeaked out.

She nodded her acceptance of his apology. The truth was she'd been called worse. Frankly, she'd barely even registered the insult.

"It's okay, Luke," she said softly. "You can

let him go." It was long past time for this train wreck to end.

All she wanted was for Nick and Jarod to leave so that she could be alone with Luke again. Her lips were still tingling from his kiss.

She wanted more.

So much more.

With what was obviously great reluctance, Luke dropped Nick's shirt and let him stumble backward into the hall.

"Come on, man," Jarod said. "There's still time to pick someone else up if we hurry."

Luke slammed her front door shut so hard she half expected the neighbors to come knocking to make sure she was okay.

"What the fuck were you doing with them?"

He looked so angry, almost disgusted, that it kicked all of her defensive urges into gear.

It was her life, thank you very much. And until tonight, he hadn't seemed to care one way or another what she did with it.

Crossing her arms over her chest, she glared back at him. "Exactly what you think."

"Jesus." The word was more of a curse than any of his earlier "fucks" or "assholes" were. "You were going to take two of them."

Before she could tell him that while that was her initial intention, she wasn't actually going to follow through on it, he had her shoulders gripped hard in his hands again.

He didn't press her up against his body this time. Instead, she was totally immobilized by his strength. She'd known he was in great shape, that his muscles were cut and ripped, but now that she was getting to know the feel of his hands on her, the truth was he was so much stronger than she'd thought.

"How many times have you done it?"

Looking up at his beautiful face, she got snared in his green eyes, and any chance she had of speaking was lost.

"Tell me, damn you. How many three-ways have you had?"

Forcing her brain to process his gritty request, she finally got out, "None."

His eyes flashed with relief a split second before wariness—and disbelief—took over. His hands tightened on her shoulders again. "Don't lie to me."

Okay, now that just made her mad. How dare he accuse her of lying!

Going on her tippy toes so that her face was barely an inch from his, she spoke each word distinctly. "I. Don't. Lie."

She always told the truth. Even when it hurt. Even when it would be so much better to spin out an easy lie.

There was a heavy pause where his eyes held hers and she thought he was going to kiss her again. She held her breath waiting for it.

Instead he said, "You were going to do it. Tonight."

She was surprised to see more than anger in his gaze. There was jealousy there, too. And concern. Had he actually been afraid for her safety?

A part of her wanted to push out of his arms and defend herself and tell him that she'd gotten out of far stickier situations with no problems. But another part—the part that had needed Luke for too damn long—had her moving closer to him and saying, “I was just about to send them home, Luke. I thought I could do it. I thought I wanted to do it. But I didn't. I couldn't.”

How could I enjoy having a three-way with a couple of strangers when the only person I really want is you?

Chapter Three

Janica Ellis was one of the most vibrant, self-confident, overtly sexual women he'd ever met. Even though she was only five years younger than he was, she'd always struck him as too young. Too raw. Way too out in the open. He didn't date girls like her, didn't see the point when it was clear that there was no future in it.

As he held her body close to his, Luke had to wonder how Janica and Lily could possibly be related. Because even though they looked nothing like each other—Lily was tall and curvy and soft with flowing red curls while Janica was small, all angles and lines with jet black hair—their differences stretched far beyond the physical.

Lily, Luke's best friend from elementary school, was the most giving, caring, loyal person he'd ever known.

Whereas everything about Janica screamed TAKE.

And yet, she was the only person he could face tonight. Was it because she was the only person he knew who wouldn't judge him—or feel a speck of pity—over the fact that his world was imploding?

Or, he had to ask himself, still tasting her

sweetness on his lips, was it simply about sex?

Hot, sweaty, slippery sex.

From the moment his lips had touched hers, his dick had been rock hard. It was sick for his sister-in-law, someone he'd known since she was in pigtails – and had told himself he didn't much liked - to give him a woody. Lord knew that was what he'd been telling himself for the past five years. But none of that mattered right now.

He was sick of being the good guy all the time. He was exhausted from fighting his desire for Janica. And he was done not taking what she gave so freely to anyone else with a heartbeat.

Sick. And getting sicker by the second. He knew it. And on any other night he would have fought against his baser urges, the way he usually did. He would have put nobility first and lust second. But he was too tired, too burnt out, too skeptical about the whole damn world and his part in it to bring himself to care, to stop the train he was on before it slammed into a brick wall.

A beautiful, erotic brick wall.

His cock shot up another inch beneath the zipper of his jeans as he drank her in, forcing everything that had happened in the ER out of his head.

Watching him watch her, Janica's eyes flashed a mixture of confusion and desire. And then, in a flash, the uncertainty disappeared, replaced with her usual feisty attitude.

He held her challenging gaze, silently acknowledging that they hadn't had an easy relationship since their siblings got married. They'd been forced together for countless lunches, dinners, and holidays, and the truth was he'd never gone out of his way to be particularly nice to her. Not when he'd made up his mind about Janica years ago in defense of his best friend, Lily, deciding that Janica was a selfish little girl who took everything she could from her older sister and rarely gave anything back.

A voice in the back of his head said, *Are you sure that's why you stayed away from her? Or were you afraid that if you ever let yourself have a taste of heaven, you wouldn't be able to pull yourself away from her? Because you just might find out that you like her more than you want to.*

What the hell was wrong with him tonight? Why was his brain playing tricks on him?

He needed to shut off the voice of reason that said to get the fuck out while he still had his pants on and stick with the plan. What had happened in the trauma center tonight had made him a different man. One he wasn't sure he'd like in the morning, but one who knew exactly what he wanted.

Janica.

He wanted her more than he'd ever wanted anyone, or anything, his whole life.

For the first time in thirty-five years he was completely lacking in moral fiber. But what did it really matter in the end? His twin, Travis, had been the biggest dog Luke knew. And even though he'd simply used women for their bodies, disrespecting their feelings all the while, he'd found true love with Lily anyway. Now he had a wife. Kids. A family.

Travis had real happiness.

What had being the good guy ever gotten Luke?

A couple of "perfect" girlfriends that he hadn't been able to fall in love with, no matter how hard he tried. And a job that was slowly killing him.

The dark side reeled him in and he no longer bothered trying to resist.

"Everything's different tonight," he told Janica and when she simply said, "Yes," then kissed him, her mouth on his was all it took to seal his deal with the devil.

Luke Carson's saint days were through.

Chapter Four

Janica couldn't get enough of Luke.

She could feel the warmth of his skin beneath his clothes as her hands roamed down his back, then back up and across his broad, muscular shoulders, but it wasn't good enough. She wanted to know the feel of him beneath her fingertips.

Skin on skin.

Let the love begin.

Oh yeah.

She couldn't remember ever feeling like this, so utterly consumed by a man, so frantic to get him naked, to feast her eyes and hands and mouth on every inch of his body. Sex had always been at the top of her favorite-things list, but this desire—this total, all-encompassing need—was something else entirely.

So different, in fact, that as she yanked his T-shirt out of his pants and broke their kiss long enough to pull it up over his head, she started freaking out a little bit.

Because with his torso bared before her, with all of that hard heat at her disposal to caress and run her tongue across, she wanted so many things so powerfully all at once that instead of being able to do any of them she found herself paralyzed.

Pressing her hands flat against his chest, she could feel the beating of his heart against her palms. A hard, fast pounding that mirrored her own heartbeat.

So many years she'd dreamed of this moment, so many years she'd thought it would never come, and now that it had, she felt almost frightened.

She lifted her eyes to his at the exact moment that her heart said, *I love you.*

No.

She stumbled back from Luke, or tried to, but his arms were faster than she was.

She hadn't read love in his eyes at any point so far tonight, only lust. Pure lust. And now he was saying, "Yes or no?" in a low voice that rumbled through her entire body like a sensual earthquake.

Oh god. It couldn't be true.

She couldn't be in love with Luke.

Of all the stupid things to feel for him, love was definitely the stupidest.

She swallowed hard, made herself locate her voice, which felt like it had dropped way down deep into her toes.

"To what question?"

"Tonight. This. You and me."

Ah, now she got it. He was asking her if she could forget about who they were. About their past. About how this could thoroughly complicate their future. He was asking her to make a choice between risking everything she was for this one night...or running scared from it.

She hadn't been afraid of anything for a very long time. So why, she wondered helplessly, was she afraid now?

And why had her brain actually thrown the word love into the mix?

His hands were warm on the small of her back, just above the curve of her ass. The heat of his bare chest radiated out to her as she stood in his arms. A bone-deep longing to shut her eyes and lay her head against him while he held her close hit her hard.

God, what was wrong with her tonight? Here she was on the verge of getting everything she'd ever wanted and instead of grabbing Luke with both hands, dragging him to her bedroom, and having her dirty way with him, she was freaking out.

"Yes or no?" he repeated.

She tried to say yes, but all she could get out was, "You already know the answer."

He shook his head, just as she'd known he would. He wasn't the kind of man you could fool. He was too smart. Too quick.

"I want to hear you say it, Janica. I need to hear you say it."

His need rocked through her. She couldn't say no to him. Just as she couldn't say no to herself, to her own desperate need.

She licked her lips. Opened her mouth. Finally whispered, "Yes."

That one small word was all it took for him

to take over. His hands moved so fast from her back to the low neckline of her short black dress that her breath caught in her throat.

Through the thin fabric she could feel his hands on the curves of her breasts and her nipples beaded almost painfully. Because she was small enough to let the built-in bra in the dress do the work of keeping everything in place, her nipples jutted out at him, silently begging him to touch her.

A split second later, he ripped the front of her dress open, fully exposing her breasts to his hungry eyes.

She gasped in shock. Who was this man, she wondered as she instinctively moved to cover herself.

Before she could, his hands camc around her wrists to hold her arms at her sides.

"No. Let me see you." His chest was rising and falling hard. "I've waited so damn long."

His eyes burned her skin, causing a flush to travel all across her breasts. But the heat did nothing to stop her nipples from hardening further.

"My God, you're beautiful."

No one had ever looked at her this way, like she was absolutely, impossibly perfect.

"So beautiful, Janica, I can't believe it."

She tried to say something but she still couldn't catch her breath. Not with her dress ripped open to her waist. Not with Luke's eyes drinking her in. Not with those wonderful things coming from his mouth.

Not with her wrists immobilized by his

strong grip.

And then he was bending his head down and she felt the first flutter of his soft hair against her collarbone as he lowered his mouth down over one breast.

A low, uncontrollable moan of pleasure shook her throat. She wanted to put her hands on the back of his head, hold him there forever against her, but he wouldn't let her go.

All she could do was stand there and let him taste her.

Oh my god. His tongue. And then—yes, yes, yes!—his teeth were lightly scoring her sensitive flesh.

"Luke."

His name was a plea. For mercy.

Or maybe, for the exact opposite.

And that was when she realized he understood her better than she did herself, because instead of letting up, instead of giving her a chance to catch her breath, he shifted his dangerous attention from one breast to the other.

The touch of his lips, his tongue, the dark stubble on his jaw, stroking across her untouched skin, sent another jolt of pure desire through her, head to toe, strong enough that she didn't know how her body was managing to hold it all inside without breaking apart.

She arched into his mouth to get closer, every cell in her body focused on three square inches. His jaw was covered in rough stubble and she loved the way it felt as it scraped and scratched against her skin.

And then his mouth was traveling up over the small curves of her breasts, across her collarbone, settling in the hollow. His tongue tasted her there, and it struck her that feeling Luke's kiss on her shoulder was one of the most erotic moments of her life, outranking every orgasm she'd ever had with anyone else.

She wanted to taste him too, wanted to run her hands and mouth over every inch of his beautiful body. But he was still holding her too tight.

She tried to pull herself out of his bonds and his hands tightened on her wrists.

He pulled his mouth away from her skin. His eyes were dark, dangerous.

"Don't fight me. Not tonight."

It wasn't just the sensual spell he had wound around her or the look in his eyes that had her giving in. It was the fact that those five words, said in such a commanding voice, held not only more desire than she'd ever known, but also more pain.

Luke needed her.

She'd never been the kind of woman who looked for broken men to try and heal. But Luke wasn't just any man. He had always been special. Even when she wished he wasn't.

"Okay," she whispered. "I won't."

Pleasure flared in his eyes, but instead of his mouth coming down on hers again, hot and hard and hungry, he released her wrists and a moment later his strong, warm fingers were stroking her hair, the tops of her shoulders, the backs of her arms. Like a cat, she rubbed against his hands.

For how rough he'd been with her dress, considering how tightly he'd held her to him, now his touch was gentle. But still all-consuming.

And with the real world completely suspended on its axis for one night, it was the most natural thing in the world to look at him and say, “I've always thought you were so beautiful.”

But it wasn't enough to say it, she had to feel his beauty, had to get inside it, become a part of it. She raised her hands to his face, pressed her thumb to his lips, her other hand stroking the light stubble across his jaw. More words floated into her brain and she knew how good it would feel to say them aloud.

“I've wanted to touch you for so long, from the first moment I saw you.”

She waited for a flash of regret at telling him a truth she'd hidden from him for so long, but it never had a chance to come. Not when his eyes were burning with desire as he looked down at her, his hands now at the small of her back, pulling her even closer. And then he was turning his face into her hand, his tongue brushing against the tip of her thumb.

Her heart raced beneath his lips as he moved to circle the pulse point on her wrist with his tongue. She could feel herself melting deeper into him, completely losing the thread of where she ended and he began.

She shivered almost violently at the pleasure

of it, closing her eyes and sinking deeper into the wonder of being with Luke.

Thinking how much she wanted this, how good it felt, the word, "Finally," left her lips.

Going up onto her toes, she stretched her neck up so that she could rub her cheek against his. And again, that innocent brush of skin against skin, jaw against jaw, was one of the most sensual experiences of her life.

She wanted more.

More. More. More.

Utterly overwhelmed by the waves of ecstasy washing over her, she realized that she was already right there, on the verge of climax.

So good.

Better than she could ever remember feeling. With nothing but his mouth on her wrist, one hand on her hip, his taut muscles pressed along hers, she was nearly at the peak, on the verge of falling over the edge at the slightest additional provocation.

Amazingly, at the same time, she felt that she could hang in this moment forever, sensually suspended in time.

It was instinctive for her to try to grind herself against him, to try and crest the peak that was right there before her. She'd always been in charge of her own pleasure, and none of her lovers had ever tried to get between her and a climax.

But Luke clearly wasn't like any lover she'd ever had, because instead of helping her come, he moved her wrists back to his hands and shifted her away from him, just far enough that she was left panting with need, close enough to the edge to practically be able to taste it.

She opened her mouth to beg him to let her come, but with only a look he reminded her that she had promised not to fight him.

And, God, it was a turn-on to let him be in control.

"I want you naked," he growled and she would've ripped her dress all the way off, but he still held her firm. And then, he was kneeling before her, pressing his mouth into her bare stomach, dipping his tongue quickly against her exposed belly button.

"So damn beautiful," she heard him murmur again against her skin.

It felt like all the blood in her body was pooling between her legs. She was throbbing, aching.

Just the thought of Luke stripping off her panties had moisture slipping and sliding from her body. But, shockingly, it seemed he wasn't in a hurry anymore. Leisurely, his mouth moved across her stomach, his lips sucking, his tongue sliding against first one hip bone and then the other.

With nothing but the gentle press of Luke's mouth against her belly, she was nearly there.

Frustrated by his slow pace, she silently begged him to move his mouth lower, lower, lower while she rocked her pelvis against him.

"Please," she begged. "That isn't where I need you."

But he acted as if he hadn't heard her plea and as his tongue continued its slow swirls of pleasure against her skin, she remembered the look in his eyes when he'd begged her not to fight him tonight.

Her thoughts swirled in a jumbled fog of arousal, her brain working so much slower than it usually did, as if she wasn't taking in enough oxygen.

Was this what he meant when he'd asked her if she was ready for 'this'? Had he been asking her if she could physically withstand letting him tease her mercilessly?

And did he expect her to hand over complete control of her body to him?

But as his mouth continued to kiss and taste and nip at the skin across her stomach, she realized that none of the answers really mattered. She'd been waiting for five years – no, a decade or more - for this moment to come to fruition. And now that it was here, she would willingly walk down whatever path he wanted to lead her down.

Deep down, she knew that Luke Carson was destined to give her great pleasure. Bigger and better than she had ever dreamed was possible.

And, if dreams really did come true, maybe he'd give her even more than pleasure.

Maybe he'd give her love.

Finally lulled into Luke's new slow pace, into the dreamlike state of being held steady by his hands and rocking her abdomen softly against his sweet mouth, into the fantasy of loving and being loved, she wasn't at all prepared for him to abruptly drop her wrists and rip her dress completely in two.

LOVE ME *by Bella Andre*

Chapter Five

Luke had never seen anything—or anyone—more arousing.

With Janica nearly naked before him, he remained on his knees and looked his fill. She was thin, but not at all too thin, her hips curving out slightly from her small waist, her breasts exactly the right size for his hands. His mouth. For him to slide his cock between.

Later, he silently told his cock, which leapt at the idea of getting near her breasts.

At getting near her period.

Beneath her dress, now messily ripped down the middle and lying on the wood floor, she wore only a thin pair of silk panties. His moment of surprise over the daisy yellow fabric—he had assumed they'd be black or blood red to go along with the oversexed image she put out, rather than a sweet patch of innocence—barely had time to catch hold in his brain.

Because the only thing he could see, now, was the darkly damp spot just where her panties covered her labia.

His instinct to touch her there was so strong that before he could assess the action, weigh it, before he could decide if it should be his next move or not in this crazy, erotic game he and Janica were playing, he was running the pad of his thumb gently over her covered mound.

Her heat seared him as she moaned and pressed her hips into his hand.

"Yes. Please. Luke," she begged. "Right there."

Barely able to hear her over the blood roaring loudly in his ears, he hooked his thumbs into the side straps of her underwear and pulled them down just a little bit.

Leaving her panties covering her labia—Jesus, he'd never teased himself with a naked woman like this, never wanted to reveal her as if she were his very last Christmas present ever so he had to make it last and last—he slid one hand around to cup her ass, while the other began its descent down into the top of the damp yellow fabric.

His four fingers covered her neatly trimmed, soft pubic hair, damp from her arousal and the intense heat of her body. As slowly as he could, wanting to savor every single moment, he slid his hand lower, until his fingers were barely covering her clit.

He heard the breath leave her body in a soft gasp, felt her hands come to the tops of his shoulders to hold herself steady.

He held his hand there, just over the top of her swollen nub and it was as if her heart had stopped beating in her chest and was now only beating between her legs. One after the other he felt the hard thud of her heartbeat through her clitoris on his fingertips. The slick arousal seeping against the tips of his fingers gave proof to the intensity of her desire.

Sweet lord, he never wanted to forget this moment when he'd touched her for the first time. For so many years he'd pushed this urge away, had tried to deny how much he wanted her. But so many nights, she'd been there in his dreams.

Just like this, only imagination instead of flesh and blood woman.

He lifted his gaze to her face and what he saw in her face rocked him to the core. Her eyes were closed and she was flushed with pleasure. He'd never seen anything as beautiful as Janica looked right then.

But more than anything else, he was struck by how right she looked standing there, nearly naked.

In his arms.

Panic slithered beneath his skin. What was he doing, feeling so much? He'd come to bash down his demons for one night, to lose himself in her body. Not to fall in-

Shit. No. He had to get back on track. Had to keep his focus on her body. On his throbbing cock.

Not on either of their hearts.

He began to move his hand again, one slow centimeter at a time, further down her labia. She was soaking wet and so obviously sensitive to his

touch that although she wasn't speaking any distinct words, he could hear her giving soft voice to her pleasure above him, one continuous low moan of ecstasy.

Suddenly, an image flashed into his head. It was so clear, so powerful, and so certain to keep him focused on sex and only sex, that even as the thought came that it wasn't fair for him to use her like this, that she hadn't ever asked him to come into her home and use her as his sexual plaything, he was yanking her panties down to her knees, and shoving her thighs open as wide as they would go with her legs still bound by the thin yellow fabric.

A heartbeat later, he had his mouth on her clit and two fingers inside her slick canal.

His cock throbbed hard once, then twice, and he thought he just might come right then and there. He'd never loved the taste of a woman more. She tasted like sugar and honey. Like heaven, even as he knew the hard thrust of his fingers inside her was going to send him straight to hell.

Her body relaxed and opened up to him even more as he laved her clit with his tongue in rough strokes before sucking it firmly with his tongue, her hands moving into his hair as she pressed her hips harder against his mouth. And then he could feel her vaginal muscles begin to tighten and clench around his fingers, could measure the heavy weight of her clitoris against his tongue, and knew she was about to come.

More than anything, he wanted to take her over the edge. He wanted to be there with her when she cried out. Wanted to hear his name on her lips and know that he had made her feel better than anyone else ever had.

Shit. What the hell was he doing? He'd come here for simple pleasure, to take what Janica clearly gave so freely to everyone else, and had ended up on his knees in front of her.

With nothing more than a kiss, she'd made him a slave to her pleasure instead of his own.

It nearly killed him to force himself to abruptly move away from her and stand up.

Her eyes flew open and her legs trembled hard enough for her to stumble back onto the couch.

"Luke, what—"

"You're not ready yet. But I am."

She looked shocked by the words coming out of his mouth. Even as he undid his belt buckle, he felt the tug of something in his gut, a twinge that told him he was being a complete asshole, and that she didn't deserve it.

He'd always been a considerate lover, was always gentle, careful to make sure he took care of his partner's pleasure first. But tonight he wanted to know—needed to know—what it was like to have a hot, talented mouth on his cock make him come first. Before his lover.

A lover who was so ripe with arousal that she would do anything, absolutely anything he asked.

Even if he had no damn right to ask it.

Even if he was being driven by all the all wrong reasons.

Even if they both hated him in the morning.

Certain that Janica had the talented mouth he'd been craving, and that she was so close to climax she could taste it, he pointed to the wooden slats in front of his boots and pulled down his zipper.

"Get on your knees."

Chapter Six

Lying half on, half off her couch, her underwear tangled around her knees, her pussy throbbing with the desperate need to come, Janica couldn't believe what she was hearing. And from Luke Carson!

Had he really just said, *Get on your knees*?

She looked up at his face, wanting to make sure that it really was Luke standing before her, rather than some dominant stranger that had taken his place when she was on the verge of losing it beneath his mouth and fingers.

No one had ever talked to her like that before. No one had dared order her around, either in or out of bed. Not only did she run her own design firm, she took control of everything else in her life, including her lovers.

But as she lay there, staring at him, the rush of anger that should have been coming at his outright order wasn't coming. Life had never been a puzzle to Janica before. She'd never been the type to waste her time philosophizing. Her motto had always been to just "shut up and do."

Tonight, however, any which way she looked, everything was a puzzle. Not only Luke's behavior, but hers too.

Why wasn't she talking back to him? Why wasn't she informing him in no uncertain terms that she'd do whatever she wanted whenever she damn well wanted to do it?

And most of all, why did letting Luke take the reins—temporarily at least—make her feel so safe? Almost comforted. Protected.

All the while, as her brain wrestled with itself, Luke's eyes were on her, moving from her soaked pussy to her breasts and then her face.

At first glance his eyes were hard, and yet, when she looked closer, in the small spaces between heartbeats, she could see something else in their green depths. Something that made her heart clench tightly in her chest.

Luke was in pain. And it was deep. Dark.

And there was something else there, too. An emotion that she'd seen in his brother, Travis's eyes when he looked at Lily. Her heart nearly stopped beating.

She understood sex. Was perfectly comfortable to with two bodies coming together in mutual desire. But the kind of thing she was seeing in his eyes...she'd never had a man look at her like that, naked or otherwise.

His voice broke into her careening thoughts. “Now, Janica.”

She snapped to at his raw words. She'd ached for him for so long, but until tonight—until just moments ago—it had been a primarily physical ache. Now, it was an emotional one too.

But even as she thought it, she knew she was lying to herself. She'd gone way beyond physical with Luke years ago, even though it had only been one-sided.

Shifting on the couch, she tried to get up to go to him, but her legs were still tangled up in her half-off panties. Moving to slide them off the rest of the way, she was stilled by Luke's commanding voice.

"Leave them."

Her nipples peaked even more at his words, at the picture she knew she was presenting to him, bound by her damp underwear, so enslaved by her own lust for him that she would do anything he asked.

Anything at all

Licking her lips, she took a breath to prepare to fight her instincts, which were surely going to tell her to battle him. But, again, nothing came.

Because, as she realized with a shocked jolt of awareness, she wanted to do exactly what he told her to.

Suddenly, fear roiled through her. Not at what Luke wanted from her—Lord knew she'd fantasized about taking him into her mouth a hundred times—but at how badly she wanted to give herself over to him.

No!

She couldn't do it.

All her life she'd taken care of herself. Because she'd had to. If she stopped now, if she gave herself over to Luke, then what would she lose hold of next?

Pushing herself back into the couch, she started shaking her head as she said, "I ca—"

But when she looked up at him again, the rest of her words caught in her throat. He wasn't saying a word, but it was almost as if she could hear his thoughts as he watched her struggle with herself.

Tonight, this, what we're doing, won't change anything. You'll still be you and I'll still be me. I'm only asking you to give me one night. I'm only asking you to give me this. And then tomorrow everything will go back to normal.

Lord, how she wanted to believe it, wanted to believe that come morning she'd be back in complete control of her world, of her place in it. That she'd be back in control of herself. And her heart. Just as she always had been.

And wasn't it the truth that if she ran from him now, if she ran from what she was feeling, all it would do was prove just how out of control she was?

Of course she could do this, of course she could let Luke lead their erotic dance for one night without losing herself. She was strong enough not to lose herself in him, in his needs.

In her own needs.

Still, getting up off the couch and moving toward him, her legs partially bound by fabric, wasn't the easiest thing she'd ever done. Not just because it was physically awkward, but because of the ongoing fight she was having with her pride the entire way.

Until the moment he dropped his pants and boxers to the floor. And she saw the most beautiful cock in the world.

He was so thick.

And so wide.

And so long.

She'd seen cocks in all shapes and sizes and colors. But Luke's was...

She shivered. There were no words for it. Nothing that would do him justice, anyway.

She was so completely focused on his erect shaft, pointing upright, almost laying against his stomach, that it was almost an afterthought to realize that she was now standing in front of him. Not taking her eyes off of his penis, she instinctively dropped to her knees.

Reverently, she raised one hand to him to touch him softly with the pad of her index finger. She ran it down the shaft, over the raised veins, felt them throb beneath her light touch.

He was so hot, velvety smooth skin stretched over steel.

So beautiful.

And all hers.

For one night.

Salivating at the thought of tasting him, of running her tongue up, down, and around his cock, she forced herself to take it slow by wrapping her hand around his huge shaft first. Her hands were fairly average-sized for a small woman, but even once she added her second hand above the first, she didn't come close to spanning the full length.

Finally, she raised her eyes and found him staring down at her with such desire it literally took her breath away. Unable to do anything but react, she tightened her grip on his shaft. His arousal slipped out and onto her fingers.

"Use your mouth."

His words were gritty and filled with stark need, less a demand now than a plea of his own.

Didn't he already know that nothing could have stopped her from taking him in her mouth? Still, there was something impossibly sexy about his telling her what to do. And when to do it.

Just this once.

Tonight with Luke, all rules were off.

Which worked perfectly for a woman who had never much cared for following the rules.

A moment later she was leaning in closer, breathing in the clean, heady scent of his arousal, and then hot, hard flesh was on her tongue and she was taking him into her mouth, opening up as wide as she could to accommodate not only his thick head but the wide shaft that followed as well.

His hands had threaded through her hair, holding her against him. Her hands were on his thighs and his quadriceps bunched and tightened beneath her fingertips with every inch deeper that she managed to take him into her throat. With gentle pressure, he rocked himself further into her and she made herself relax the muscles in her throat to take even more.

Just looking at him, she'd known it would be impossible to take his entire shaft. Her lips and throat had never been stretched like this. What, she wondered wildly as her body gushed arousal, was it going to feel like to take him inside her pussy?

Her mouth still on him, she groaned at the delicious thought of his cock stretching her wide. His penis throbbed hard once, then twice in her mouth. His fingers tightened in her hair.

"Don't do that again," he growled. "Hell, don't even move."

Suddenly, she could taste more of him, and knew that her inadvertent groan must have reverberated all around him.

Feeling wicked, she hummed really, really softly. His cock moved in her mouth, and she tasted him again.

God, he was delicious.

A heartbeat later, her mouth was empty.

Still on her knees, she watched him yank off his shirt, take off his shoes, and shed his pants and boxers completely.

Wow.

After already seeing his cock, she felt like she should have been prepared for his naked body, that it shouldn't come as such a hard erotic shock to see all those muscles, all that dark skin.

But she wasn't ready. And it was a shock.

She'd spent the past ten years working with models, both female and male. But she'd never seen this.

Luke Carson was perfect.

Belatedly realizing she was sitting there with her mouth hanging open, she gave him a saucy little smile. "Now that I've started to get used to how big you are," she paused, licking her lips, "I bet I can do even better than that."

But instead of stepping closer and shoving himself back into her willing mouth, he reached down and picked her up, one arm sliding beneath her legs, the other around her back, and headed down the hall, obviously looking for her bedroom.

"Later. I need to fuck you. Now."

LOVE ME *by Bella Andre*

Chapter Seven

"Condoms."

As she twisted her torso to reach for her bedside table, he pulled her panties off and threw them across the room.

If he didn't get inside her in the next sixty seconds, he was going to fucking lose it.

She ripped open the packet and reached out to put it on him but he knew he was already so far gone that if she so much as touched him, he would blow. Yanking it out of her hands, he gritted his teeth as he shoved the condom down over his throbbing dick.

And then he was crawling over her and she was reaching for him.

Goddamn it, all he wanted to do was to shove himself deep inside her and never come back out.

But even in his feverish state, where black had turned to white and white to black, he knew he couldn't do that.

He was too big. He'd hurt her.

God, he didn't want to hurt her.

He wanted to love her.

His cock head poised just at her slick

opening, he stilled at the shocking thought.

What the hell was he doing bringing love into this? Into tonight?

Whatever happened, he had to remember that being with Janica was nothing more than sex.

Nothing more than release.

Nothing more than a way to clear his head.

She moved beneath him and shifted her hips up to try and take him inside and all reminders, all thoughts entirely fell away.

Bracing himself above her, he said, “Look at me,” knowing there was no way he could just take her like she was any other woman.

No matter how much he wanted to pretend otherwise, she was special.

And he had to make sure that he took care of her.

Her eyes flew to his. “Please, take me, Luke.”

It took every ounce of remaining control that he had not to drive himself into her. But he couldn't. Not if meant there was the slightest chance of his hurting her.

“We're going to do this slow. Easy.”

She didn't argue with words, she simply used her body instead by bucking her hips forcefully up into him.

He sucked in a hard breath as his head pushed into her slick heat. Even though the latex cover he could feel how hot, how wet she was. Nothing had ever felt this good. He wanted to rip the condom off and sink into her, skin on skin. But that was something reserved for a relationship. For commitment.

Not for a one night stand.

And just as he had suspected, he was far too thick to simply slide in the rest of the way. Even as wet and aroused as she clearly was, she'd need to get used to the size of his shaft and open up to him little by little.

She closed her eyes, but he needed her to keep them open so that he could watch her and make sure he wasn't hurting her.

She was so small. So perfect. He couldn't stand the thought of hurting her.

"Open for me, sweetheart."

Her eyes flew open, wide and stunned.

It had been so natural to call her sweetheart that he almost hadn't noticed he'd done it. Now, he found himself holding himself up on one arm so that he could reach up and brush his fingers against her beautiful face.

He felt it then, the gentle easing of her inner muscles, and as he bent down to press his lips against hers, he slowly moved deeper.

He took her gasp of pleasure into his own lungs as he continued to slide in. Further and further he went, feeling her widen her legs beneath him even further, until she had taken more than half of his shaft.

He needed to stop, needed to make sure that she was okay, but for the first time in his life, he was all out of control. He needed to be in her, to the hilt, no matter what.

And then her ankles came around his hips, and she whispered, "I want all of you," against his mouth a split second before she pushed his hips hard into hers with her legs.

For such a small woman, she was much stronger than he ever would have thought, almost strong enough to get what she wanted.

What they both wanted.

Despite his attempt at control, he slid in another inch, and then another. He could feel her heated flesh holding his erection so tightly that even breathing was enough at this point to send him over the edge as her tight inner muscles contracted against his painfully hard dick.

Finally, he accepted that there was no more holding back.

No more trying to be in control.

He had to take her.

Had to make her completely, irrevocably his.

And as she pushed her tongue against his, he thrust himself all the way into her.

His amazed realization—*Jesus, she's taking all of me*—was utterly secondary to the sensation of being wrapped so tightly in such snug warmth.

Her mouth had been spectacular, but her pussy was a goddamned miracle.

Pulling back from her mouth, he had to look at her, had to see the woman who was doing this to him, who was taking him apart from the inside out.

Her eyes were open as she looked at him as if in wonder, her pupils dilated with pleasure, and she was so beautiful.

So incredibly beautiful.

Not able to take his eyes from hers, moving as slowly as he could with the blood boiling in his veins, he began the slow slide back and then forward again. With every stroke her body opened up to his a little bit more, a flood of fresh arousal lubricating his path inside of her.

He'd never felt pleasure like this. Had never known a woman to be so strong and yet soft all at the same time. Had never wanted to look into someone's soul and know that there was a place for himself there.

Because he swore that's what he saw when he looked into her eyes.

A hundred times over the next minutes as they moved together, he could have come. Explosively. But, goddamn it, now that he was where he'd thought he wanted to be, right there on the verge of exploding in her willing body, all he wanted was to give her pleasure.

Knowing it was going to nearly kill him to leave her body, he forced himself back into the cool air.

Her eyes were unfocused with pleasure. And now, confusion. "Luke?"

"You're beautiful," he said against her lips, before taking them in a quick, hard kiss.

"So are you. Please fuck me some more."

A smile moved onto his face before he even realized it was coming. "I will. After you come."

She shook her head frantically. "No. Please. I want you inside of me again."

Lord, he wanted to be inside her again too, but he needed to give her this first. “Not before you come, sweetheart.”

“I can come like that.”

About to kiss his way down her sweat-dampened naked body, he stilled and held her gaze. Another smile, this one full of sensual promise, came with his response.

“Good. Then you'll come around my cock the second time.”

At her swift intake of breath, he moved his lips and hands quickly over her sweet breasts and rock-hard nipples, down across her belly, then slid his mouth back over her mound. Her clit was a hard nub against his tongue. Knowing he couldn't bear this torture for much longer, he sucked her into his mouth at the same time that he slid first one finger, then two into her hot passage.

She cried out his name as she arched into his mouth. And this time when he felt her inner muscles tighten on his fingers, instead of pulling away, he focused in on her swollen, heated flesh.

Her entire body tightened beneath his hands, the tendons in her thighs tightening around his head, as she circled in on her orgasm. He felt the rapid spasming of her vaginal muscles clamping down on his fingers a split second before her cry of pleasure sounded into her bedroom.

Jesus, she was tight. And strong. Knowing he was about to be back inside of her, knowing she was going to come again around his cock, knowing that she was all his for at least one night, had him almost climaxing onto her bed cover.

He'd never moved as fast as he did right then, to get back inside her, and—fuck!—as soon as he pushed his head inside of her, he realized she was even tighter, even hotter, even wetter now that he'd finally let her come.

Thank God at least he knew he wasn't going to hurt her, because he couldn't hold back this time.

Letting loose all the pent up lust for Janica that he'd carefully corralled for the past five years, maybe even longer than that, he drove himself into her, high and hard. Her slick flesh stretched open for him before closing back in a perfectly snug clasp around his thick, pulsing cock. She was still coming, her muscles grasping him in rhythmic bursts as he thrust into her again and again.

Her eyes were squeezed tightly shut as she took everything he gave her and somehow managed to give it back in equal measure.

He'd never fucked a woman like this. Never taken anyone's pussy so ruthlessly.

As if she could read his mind, Janica hissed, "Harder, Luke. Please. Harder," her hands gripping his shoulders tightly, her legs wrapped tight around his waist.

His balls tightened almost painfully at her desperate appeal and it was pure instinct to take her ankles in his hands and push her legs up high, so that they were resting on his shoulders. There'd been too much of a risk of hurting his previous lovers with deep penetration to ever do the position justice, but something told him Janica could not only take him like this, but that it would give her at least as much pleasure as it gave him.

Her back walls pressed hard into his cock as he rammed into her fully open body, and he swore he could feel his head pushing against her womb.

He was right there, about to shoot his load into the most beautiful woman he'd ever known, when he saw the moisture coming from the corners of her eyes.

No!

He'd hurt her.

"Oh God, Janica, I'm sorry," he said, his words all rushing together as he tried to get his body to obey his brain and get out of her incredibly hot, tight body.

The tiny body he was ripping in two.

But before he could do anything at all, her hands were on his face.

"I love you, Luke." More tears flowed, making her next words thick as she said again, "I love you so much."

Her declaration was one thing too many for him to process and even as his body took in more stimuli than it ever had before, he could feel his brain—and heart—starting to shut down.

But then, somehow, he was wiping away her tears and she was turning her face into his palm and gently kissing the inside of his hand. His body started moving again, driving back in, then out of her in hard strokes, completely of its own volition.

"Love me, Luke," she begged him, and then they were shifting on the bed so that her body was pressed lengthwise against his and her legs were coming around his hips again and she was pulling his mouth down onto hers and he was kissing her like he'd never kissed another woman.

Like she was his first, his last, and everything in between.

And then, with her tongue stroking his, her hands warm and strong on his back, he detonated with a roar of pleasure, any thoughts of hurting her obliterated beneath his explosive release. Somewhere in there he realized she was coming again, crying out his name as her body tensed then released in ecstasy.

Making love to Janica Ellis was beyond amazing. Worlds better than incredible.

Being with her was simply mind-blowing.

But later, what struck him as the most amazing thing of all was not that she'd been able to take all of him and then some.

It wasn't even that she'd used the word "love."

It was how right it was to pull her into his arms, how good it felt to have her curl into the protective curve of his body.

And how natural and easy it was to fall immediately into the deep, healing sleep he so desperately needed.

Chapter Eight

Luke woke to a dark bedroom.

Janica's bedroom.

Apart from the fact that she must have gotten up to turn off the light at some point, they hadn't moved for hours. Still curled into his body, Janica's breathing was even, her back to his chest. Her ass was softly pressing against his groin, her breasts resting against his forearm.

He didn't need time to react to her warm, naked body. He was already there, as hard and ready as if he hadn't already fucked her senseless.

He couldn't have gotten more than three or four hours of sleep and yet he felt better than he did after a full night's rest.

Almost as if being with Janica had restored him in some elemental way.

Shifting slightly in her sleep, her butt cheeks slid against his cock. His body wanted badly to take over, to shift her another inch so that he could experience all of that slick warmth again.

He'd never wanted anything more than to take her again.

She shifted again, almost right where he wanted her, but just as he was about to give in to his baser desires, just as he had only hours ago, he suddenly heard her voice in his head, as clearly as if she were speaking aloud.

I love you, Luke.

If she hadn't said those words to him, if he could have pretended she was no different than any other woman he'd been with...

Fuck.

She wasn't just anyone. She was his best friend's little sister. She was his sister-in-law.

And she thought she was in love with him.

What had he done?

* * *

Janica felt Luke shift beside her as he worked to slide his arm out from beneath her frame.

Her heart started pounding. Hard.

In the real world where things made sense and she stayed on one side of the playground while Luke stayed on the other, she knew he was right to leave. That whatever had happened between them was all wrong.

But, God, it had felt so right.

Better than right.

Perfect.

And in the dark, in the aftermath of those moments when he'd called her sweetheart and looked into her eyes as if he really and truly cared about her, all she knew was that she would die inside if he left.

"Stay."

He stilled, like a thief caught in the act.

And maybe he was a thief, she thought. Because somehow, when she wasn't looking, he'd snuck in and stolen her heart.

Damn him.

Seductively, instinctively, she rubbed herself against him so that his rock-hard shaft slid between her already slick labia, the soft curve of her butt cheeks. Reaching around for one of his hands, she placed it over one of her breasts.

Her nipple beaded against his large hand and she could feel him pulsing against the flesh between her thighs, still tender from his wonderfully rough lovemaking.

A few more seconds and, oh please, his incredible cock would be sliding back into her pussy and she could experience pure ecstasy for a second time.

Only, the next thing she knew she was alone in her bed.

And the worst part of it was that he didn't say anything. He simply pulled away from her and walked naked out of her bedroom.

Stunned, she lay there for a moment, cold without his arms around her, empty without his thick heat driving into her.

Fortunately, anger came fast on the heels of her shock.

Jumping off the bed, she rushed into her living room to see that Luke was almost fully dressed already.

"You're leaving."

His face was an impenetrable mask. "Yes."

So that was the way it was going to be?

Fine. She didn't want any apologies from him. And she definitely didn't want his thanks for a killer fuck.

He hadn't taken anything from her that she hadn't wanted to give.

Except, a small voice in her head whispered, *quite possibly, her heart.*

Sixty seconds later, he was gone.

* * *

Luke went home, showered, then headed straight back to the hospital.

One of his colleagues had to need a break, had to have a shift he could fill. As long as he stayed busy he could keep himself from going there, back to Janica's apartment, back to the moment when she'd glared at him and said, *You're leaving.*

What she'd really meant was, *Fuck you.*

Even after his shower, he swore he could scent her, as if her beautiful essence had slipped past his skin, all the way into his cells. His cock thickened beneath his scrubs and he worked like hell to douse his growing hard-on, which was completely inappropriate for a doctor to be sporting. But he had to work even harder to crush that twinge in his gut that told him he'd been a complete asshole.

And that she'd deserved a hell of a lot better of a goodbye than he'd given her.

Especially since he hadn't said goodbye at all. He'd just left like a fucking coward.

Trying to focus his vision on the staffing board, he was about to call Bonnie to tell her not to bother coming in, when Eileen Jones, the hospital's head psychiatrist said, "Good morning, Luke. You're just the person I wanted to see. Would you mind coming into my office for a quick chat?"

He was barely in her door when she hit him with, "You're too tired. You need to take some time off."

"I'm fine," he shot back. Quickly realizing he needed to back off the defensive or she'd definitely think something was up, he sat down in an open chair and put his hands behind his head.

She didn't look at all convinced. "When's the last time you slept?"

"I spent last night in bed."

Which was true. He just hadn't been sleeping.

And, sweet Lord, Janica had been hot. Better than anything he could have ever imagined.

She'd been giving, too. Selfless in her passion.

And so damn sweet, he hadn't ever wanted to let her go.

Eileen sighed loudly. "That may well be the case, and I hate having to do this, Luke, but someone has to unplug you from the operating table, because you're clearly not going to do it yourself."

Luke stood up to argue his case, but Eileen

waved him back down. "I know you're going to say that they need you—"

"They do."

"—and that you feel fine—"

"I do. I'm fine, Eileen." He held out his hands. "They're not shaking. I'm not seeing double. Or hallucinating. I don't have any signs of sleep deprivation. I've been working this way for years, and I'm responsible for saving more lives than anyone in this hospital, so I appreciate your concern but—"

She cut him off. "I know what happened last night, that Robert had to take over for you. And before you start beating yourself up over it, I want you to know I've seen it happen to all of the best doctors. So I'm not at all concerned about your patients, Luke. I'm concerned about you. You need some time off. To rejuvenate. To have some fun." Looking down at the papers on her desk she said, "You'll be taking the next four weeks off."

Four weeks? Fuck, no. How was he supposed to make it through the next twenty-four hours without his job to fall back on? Between what had happened in the ER and what had happened with Janica, he was as screwed in the head – and the heart - as he'd ever been.

"One week," he countered.

"We don't want you to set foot in the hospital for four weeks, Luke," she said firmly, the handed him his walking papers.

The words swam before him. *Mental health break.*

They thought he was going nuts.

And given that he'd spent the night trying to fuck his sister-in-law's brains out, but making love to her instead, maybe he had.

"The Big Sur cabin is open this time of year. It's yours. A few weeks on the ocean is going to work wonders for you. I'm sure of it."

Thirty minutes later, Luke was still fuming. *There's nothing wrong with my mental health*, he thought as he burned up the road beneath his tires, driving Highway 1 south too fast considering his lack of sleep. And yet, he was completely off kilter, utterly unprepared for the weeks that stretched before him.

With every mile he covered, Eileen's parting words came at him: "*You don't have to save everyone, Luke. Nobody can. And that's okay.*"

But she was wrong.

He did.

Because he hadn't been able to save the one person he'd loved the most.

LOVE ME *by Bella Andre*

Chapter Nine

Janica rang Lily's doorbell, but knowing the neighborhood was so safe they rarely locked the front door, she didn't wait for anyone to let her in.

Violet, Lily's four year-old daughter, came barreling around the corner. "Auntie Jan!" She tackled Janica in a bear hug around her legs, then yelled, "You're it," and ran away as fast as her small legs could take her.

Janica grinned. Damn, she loved that kid. A perfect cross between Lily's soft beauty and Travis's ridiculously masculine good looks, Violet was a stunner. Better still, she was funny. And bright as the sun.

Lily was kneeling in the kitchen with full grocery bags all around her feet as she consoled her crying son. Sam was almost two-and-a-half and about a hundred times more sensitive than his big sister. He was also crazy cute. Cover-of-a-kid's-magazine cute.

Hoping to distract him from whatever was the matter, Janica called out, "Sammy!"

His eyes still wet, he looked up from his mother's shoulder and in an instant his wobbling cheeks shifted into a wide smile.

"Hey, baby boy," she said as Lily gratefully moved aside to let her pick him up.

Happily going into her arms, he made a stern face. "I'm not a baby."

"I know," she said. "You're a big boy." She pretended she was going to drop under his weight. "A huge boy. Have you been eating bricks again?"

"That would make my teeth break, silly!" he crowed, happy to let her know just how wrong she was, just like his father—and his uncle—were so happy to do all the time.

Carson men. They were all alike.

Too damn cute to stay away from, but completely and utterly full of themselves.

"You're it! You're it!" Violet yelled as she ran by.

"Okay. I'm just going to tell Sammy a secret first," Janica said.

Violet's eyes got really big. Forgetting all about her game of tag, she ran over. "What is it?"

"I need to talk to your mommy for a few minutes and then when we're done I'm taking everyone for cupcakes."

Lily's little boy all but jumped out of her arms to do a happy cupcake dance with his sister.

"I want to go right now!" he demanded.

Carson boys and their demands.

Come here.

I want you naked.

Get on your knees.

Use your mouth.

She shivered at the still-potent memories of

the previous night and Lily looked at her with concern.

"Jan, honey, are you okay?"

Working to push Luke out of her head for five seconds, Janica smiled at the kids and pointed to the clock on the kitchen wall. "When the little arm is pointing at the 6, we'll go. Violet, you know how to tell time, don't you?"

Violet puffed up her chest. "Of course I do." And then she grabbed her brother's arm and said, "Let's go play bakery in my room until it's time to go. You can make me cupcakes and I can eat them."

Stepping over grocery bags, Lily hugged her quickly, then pulled her over to one of the bar stools tucked under the granite-topped island.

"What's wrong?"

Oh crap. Why had she come here? What was she thinking? Lily was going to kill her. Or Luke. Either way, her big sister was going to be worried sick over the whole situation.

But the thing was, even though Janica knew all those things, she had to talk to someone about what had happened. She needed her best friend. Who just so happened to be Luke's best friend too.

"Something happened last night."

Lily's worried look morphed into pure fear. "Are you okay?"

Janica wanted to nod, tried to say yes, but the truth was she wasn't sure she actually was okay. Luke had rocked her world so hard she hadn't just seen stars, she'd actually felt like a human kaleidoscope shifting form again and again, from formations of pinks to purples and reds, yellows and oranges, blues and greens. Her orgasm had gone on and on as if it would never end, one easily turning to two beneath his beautifully out-of-control onslaught. And for a moment she'd felt special. Cherished.

But then he'd left, at least as cold as he'd ever been to her.

Colder, even.

"Oh my God, Jan, if someone hurt you we need to go to the pol—"

Janica quickly cut her off. "No, it's nothing like that." She paused, took a deep breath, knew she needed to spit it out already before Lily had the chief of police on the line.

"Luke came over."

Lily frowned. "Luke came over?"

Janica nodded.

Lily cocked her head to the side, still clearly confused by what Luke had to do with anything. And then, suddenly, her eyes went big.

"Luke came over," Lily said again, more slowly this time, as if her brain was too busy working out the ramifications of everything to be able to change the words into anything else.

Jumping straight over the inevitable question—*did you sleep with him?*—Janica gave her sister the answer with another nod.

At which point Lily's eyes grew even huger and her cheeks flushed, her mouth opening and shutting a couple of times without any words coming out.

LOVE ME ***by Bella Andre***

Janica was glad for her sister's loss for words because it meant that she could spit out the rest of it as quickly as possible.

"The thing is, apart from the obvious, I did something really stupid."

Shaking herself out of her shock, Lily put her warm hands over Janica's cold ones. "Okay, so you slept with Luke. I know it's a big deal. A huge deal. But that doesn't mean it was stupid, Jan."

If only sex was all there was to it.

I love you, Luke. I love you so much.

How could she have said those things to him?

How could she have even thought them?

Or dared to feel them in the first place?

"It was beyond stupid," Janica insisted.

"I'm sure he's safe," Lily said softly, totally misunderstanding her comment.

"No, we used protection," Janica told her. "That's not the problem."

"Then what is it?"

She took a very shaky breath, before saying, "I told him I loved him."

The silence between the sisters was heavy. Finally, Lily whispered, "Oh, Janica," then hugged her close.

Her sister's pity made her feel a hundred times worse. As if it was starkly obvious to every last person on earth that there was no point in Janica loving Luke because they could never end up together.

"What did he say?"

Janica shook her head. He hadn't said anything. But she remembered the way his eyes had looked right after she'd said it.

Like he couldn't take it in. Not just because he hadn't been expecting her to say it.

But because he didn't want her to.

Lily's voice was gentle as she asked, "How long have you felt that way?"

Janica shrugged, not wanting to have to admit to either Lily or herself that her feelings were real. "It was really great sex."

But Lily wasn't buying it. "How many other times have you declared your love to someone you've slept with?"

Janica hated to say it. "Never."

"Do you want me to talk to him?"

"No! Absolutely not!" Janica shook her head hard. "All I want to do is forget it ever happened."

A lightning bolt coming through the roof to strike her dead just then wouldn't have surprised her in the least. Not when she'd just told the world's hugest lie.

Because she never wanted to forget her night with Luke. Lying beneath him, his hard heat filling her body and soul, his mouth on hers. It had been the most perfect night of her life. So perfect that she hadn't been able to stop three horrible words from spilling out of her lips. More than once.

"Somehow, honey, I don't think that's going to work. He's Travis's brother. Odds are, you're going to have to see him again pretty soon."

Janica put her face in her hands. "I know.

I'm so screwed."

Lily got up from the stool and started pacing. "No, I refuse to believe that. In fact, maybe it's a good thing this happened. You know, for the two of you to finally get your feelings for each other out in the open."

Janica looked up from her hands. "Hate to break it to you, Lils, but not everyone gets the fairy tale like you did."

But Lily's eyes were already bright with plans and hopes. "You're amazing. You love him. He's got to know how lucky he is. He's got to. He probably just needs some time to get used to the idea of being a part of a couple."

If ever there was a perfect moment for an eye roll, this was it. "Even for you, big sister, that is a shockingly misplaced vote of confidence. Do you really for one second think Luke wants my love? That he could even consider being with someone like me?"

Lily immediately got angry. "Don't you dare talk about yourself like that. He'd be the luckiest guy on earth to have you."

Deciding they were officially way past the eye roll, Janica simply sighed. "So in your version of reality the type A surgeon has always wanted a wild clothing designer to be his one and only?"

"He showed up at your apartment last night, didn't he?" When Janica nodded, Lily asked, "Has he ever come by before?"

"No. Not since that time you and Travis left for Italy and ended up getting married."

Five years ago, Janica and Luke had concocted a plan to make sure Lily and Travis, who clearly belonged together, didn't screw things up. It was the last time she'd ever really sat down and talked with Luke. Including last night, when words hadn't been necessary.

"He must have told you why he showed up."

"Nope."

"And you didn't ask him?"

"There wasn't exactly room for a lot of questions."

Lily pretended to put her hands over her ears. "I'm not sure I can listen to any more of the details."

Janica leaned forward on the counter and said in a hushed tone, "Well first he—"

At Lily's horrified look she started laughing, incredibly glad for the chance to feel some lightness for just a few moments. "Just kidding. You know I don't kiss and tell."

"Who's the lucky guy this time?" Travis said, walking in at the tail end of her sentence, carrying a basketball.

Lily simply lit up when she saw her husband. Janica was momentarily forgotten as Travis and Lily put their arms around each other and kissed. A little while later, Lily shot her a questioning look.

No! Janica shot back silently.

All she needed was for Travis to find out about her and Luke. Wouldn't he just love that?

She'd never ever—ever!—hear the end of it

from her pain-in-the-ass brother-in-law.

The kids came barreling into the kitchen a second later. “Daddy! Auntie Jan is taking us for cupcakes!” Violet yelled as he squatted down and she threw herself into his arms.

Sammy was right behind her. “Cupcakes! Cupcakes!”

After telling them how excited he was about their good fortune, he shot Janica a scowl. “Nothing like a bunch of sugar to really make things easy on their parents.”

“You're welcome,” she said with an unapologetic smile she knew would really irk her sister's husband.

Lily looked at the clock on the kitchen wall and frowned. “I thought you and Luke were meeting to play basketball?”

“He stood me up so I picked up a quick game with a couple of guys already there.”

Lily glanced at Janica. “Is something wrong with Luke that you haven't told me?”

Travis didn't look at all concerned as he opened the fridge and got out a bottle of orange juice. “He probably got called into the ER. You know how nuts his schedule is.”

As soon as he left to take a shower, Lily grabbed the phone. “I've got to talk to Luke, make sure he's okay.”

Janica leapt up to grab the phone out of Lily's hand. “No. Please. This is already so embarrassing. If you call him, you'll end up saying something about me. I know you will.”

"I promise I won't, Jan, but he's my best friend. I have to find out what's going on."

Less than a minute later, Lily put the phone back down on the counter. "He didn't answer at home or at work. And his cell phone said his voice mail is full. This isn't like him, Jan."

Janica already knew that. Clearly, the only reason why he'd come over to her place was because something was very, very wrong. But the sex had been too all-consuming for her to even begin to ask him any questions.

And he'd gotten the hell out of there before she could.

Lily wasn't the only one worried about Luke.

Because even though he'd walked out on her, Janica was too.

And no matter how tempting it was to try and pretend nothing with Luke had ever happened, she knew she couldn't pull it off.

Not when taking risks was what Janica did.

Not when, despite knowing better, despite the fact that her heart was only going to keep breaking apart, the truth was as simple as it came.

She really was in love with him.

Head over fucking heels.

"Violet. Sam. Let's go get cupcakes." The kids ran back into the room. "I'll bring them back when they're full to the brim with cake and frosting," she told her sister.

And then, she was going to go find Luke.

To find out what the hell was going on.

LOVE ME ***by Bella Andre***

Chapter Ten

Now she knew something was really wrong. Luke didn't take vacations. He worked.

Janica was a bit of a workaholic herself, so she got late nights and working through the weekend. But she also knew how to have fun. How to completely let go and forget everything except a good time.

The drive out to Big Sur was stunningly beautiful. She tried to picture Luke sitting in an oceanfront cabin, doing nothing but looking out at the waves.

He must be going crazy.

It hadn't been hard to find out where he was. She'd simply gone to the hospital and told a couple of doctors that she needed to talk to Luke Carson immediately. At first they had been cagey with her, until she told them that she was his sister-in-law. Perhaps it hadn't been right for her to make them assume it was a family emergency, but in a way, wasn't it? After all, she and Luke were family.

And in her worst moments since he'd left in the middle of the night, everything had kind of felt like an emergency.

Following the directions she'd been given,

she turned off Highway 1 onto a narrow gravel driveway. It wound up the mountain, then over the peak and down the other side. Blue water sparkled at her through the thick cypress trees.

She could easily imagine sitting out on one of the bluffs with her sketchpad. Already, she could see a new line of printed fabrics in greens and blues. But she wasn't here to work on new designs.

She was here for Luke.

And, if she was being completely honest, for herself too. Because if there was any chance that things could actually go somewhere between the two of them-

No. She couldn't go there. She shouldn't go there. Not when she knew better.

Didn't she?

Inner turmoil roiled inside her as she pulled in behind Luke's car in the tiny gravel parking lot. Stepping out of the car, she forced herself to take a moment to breathe in the sweet-smelling ocean air.

No one had ever called Janica stupid, and they weren't about to now. She knew exactly what she was walking into.

Luke was going to hate that she was here. He was going to hate that she knew something had gone wrong for him at the hospital. And odds were pretty damn high that he was going to take it out on her.

The question was, how?

Standing alone in the trees, looking out on the water, she smiled. Despite her nerves, the adventurous part of her was looking forward to seeing what he would do—and if they would end up together in bed again.

Walking around the side of the cabin, she saw stairs that led to a front porch. Never one to back down from a challenge, she squared her shoulders, lifted her chin, and headed up. The deck chairs and dining table were all empty, but the door was wide open. Almost as if Luke couldn't be bothered even to shut it.

Her heart racing with anticipation simply at the thought of seeing him again, she made her way across the deck to the doorway. He was sitting in the only chair that faced away from the ocean. And it looked like he had a half-empty bottle of tequila in his hands.

"Nice place they keep up here for you doctors. If I'd known that these were the perks, I might have become a doctor too."

"What the hell are you doing here?"

He asked the question without even turning to look at her. A guaranteed way to piss her off. And yet, he didn't seem particularly surprised by her presence. Almost as if he'd known she was going to come down here to find him.

She said the easiest thing first—"Lily is worried about you."—then hated herself for it.

She never took the easy way out. She wasn't going to start now.

"I'm worried about you."

Still not turning to face her, he said, "You need to go."

Good one. He had to know she wasn't going

anywhere.

Scanning the room for the seat with the best ocean view, she moved to it and sat down, kicking her legs up onto the coffee table. “I've been needing a vacation. I think I'll take it here.”

Now he had no choice but to look at her. “I don't have time for your games, Janica.”

“Actually, from what I hear, you've got nothing but time. Four weeks of time.”

In a flash, he was up on his feet and coming after her. He grabbed her shoulders and wrenched her up from her seat.

“You're leaving. Right now.”

But she wasn't afraid of him. Even if, judging by his furious expression and the extremely hard grip he had on her, she should be.

“Not until you tell me what's going on. Not until you tell me why you showed up at my place last night.”

His answer came fast, furious. “I wanted to fuck you.”

She flinched and saw a flash of regret in his eyes. But it was gone as fast as it had come.

What had happened to him? To the Luke she knew?

And why couldn't she just let him go back to living his life alone, completely separate from her?

But she already knew the answer to that.

Love.

“And now I want you to leave me the hell alone.”

There was such hardness to his words, a

lifelessness beneath them that broke her heart. Not because he was hurting her with his callousness after the night they'd spent together – even though she had to admit there was a little hurt bubbling up inside of her – but because it was clear just how much he was hurting.

Last night she'd looked into his eyes, had run her fingers across the harsh lines of his face, and knew how much he needed her. But today, things were even worse.

What had happened?

Janica knew she'd never been good with this emotion stuff. All her life, she'd been physical, active.

How could she reach him?

All she knew was that she couldn't go. She couldn't leave him alone. Not like this.

Making a show of scanning the cabin, she said, "It looks to me like you've got plenty of space here. Besides, you wouldn't turn out family, would you?"

"Don't go there, Janica," he warned her in a low, rough voice.

"Where else should I go, Luke? Would you rather I told you how much I liked it when you had your mouth on my—"

Half expecting him to bodily throw her off the porch at this point, she was surprised when he cut her off with a kiss, a hard connection of lips and tongues and teeth. He tasted like tequila and his own particular brand of heat.

How would she ever get her fill of him?

A sharp pang squeezed her heart. *She never would.*

Both of them were breathing hard when he yanked himself away, only this time she was the one who didn't want to meet his eyes.

Because, for the first time in her life, she cared too much.

And she was the one who was going to end up destroyed.

Love sucked.

Especially when it only went one way.

Especially when a little voice in her head told her there wasn't a chance in hell that Luke was ever going to return her feelings. If she were anyone else, if she was blonde and tall and arctic like all of his girlfriends had been, then maybe she would have a chance with him. But Luke Carson falling in love with Janica Ellis?

Freaking preposterous.

His eyes were dark, hard, shut down as he stared down at her. "I'll let you stay on one condition."

Suddenly, it was hard to breathe. She wanted to stay so much. Too much.

"Tell me."

"I want you naked."

Despite the ache of her heart, despite the fact that he hadn't said one nice, one kind, one gentle thing to her so far, despite the fact that he hadn't apologized for leaving her apartment the night before without a goodbye, her body instantly reacted to his command.

Wasn't this exactly what she wanted? To be naked and sweaty with him again? After all, hadn't she spent her whole life chasing pleasure?

But for some reason, she couldn't just start ripping off her clothes as if she didn't have a care in the world.

Because she did care.

And because a little part of her heart actually felt like it was breaking. This time, entirely for herself.

He leaped on her hesitation. “Take off your clothes before I do it for you.” He paused, a muscle jumping in his jaw. “Or get the hell out.”

Hardly able to believe her fingers were trembling—when was the last time she felt this nervous, this unsure?—she reached for the hem of her top and pulled it over her head. He didn't try to help, didn't rip it off of her like he had the night before. Instead, he just stood there like a he had turned to heartless stone and watched her as she unbuttoned the top of her jeans, pulled the zipper down, and slid them down her legs.

Left in only a bra and panties, strangely, she felt shy.

“Everything off, Janica.”

She swallowed, shook her head. It wasn't that he hadn't seen her naked before, because obviously he had. It was that she'd suddenly realized something truly shocking.

More hot sex with Luke wasn't going to be enough.

Not for her.

Even if he was acting like sex was the only thing he wanted from her.

She had to know that at least a small part of his heart was involved first. And if it turned out that it wasn't, well then she was going to have to do the hardest thing imaginable—she was going to have to walk away from Luke. And his incredible lovemaking.

And any chance at all of a future togeth-

Damn it. She needed to stop doing that. Needed to stop imagining that there was even the slightest chance that he could fall for her.

Still, even if he was never going to fall in love with her, she couldn't have sex with him again if there wasn't a chance at their being friends after everything was over.

After this craziness had finally come to its inevitable end.

Her heart felt like someone had been kicking it with steel-toed boots as she said, "You don't like me."

She read his surprise at her abrupt statement loud and clear. It wasn't what she planned to say, but now that she had, she couldn't hide from the truth of it.

"I like fucking you."

Oh. Wow.

That hurt.

But what had she expected him to say? *Oh no, Janica. I absolutely adore you.*

As if.

"I loved fucking you too," she said softly,

working like hell to mask her careening emotions. But she couldn't. She could feel her cheeks falling, her mouth starting to shake despite her attempts at control. “So that's all this is?”

A deep, dark anguish flashed across his face. And then, instead of answering, instead of breaking her heart the rest of the way, instead of grinding it completely to dust, he moved closer, caressed her cheek with one of his large hands.

She blinked up at Luke, knowing she should leave, telling herself to leave, but then his mouth was on hers and it was such a gentle, sweet kiss that she simply melted into him.

Thank god. She didn't have to leave him.

* * *

He wasn't alone.

Janica had dropped everything in her life to come here to be with him. She'd given her body to him, then given him her heart too, and even after he'd walked out on her the night before without one kind word, she'd gone to the hospital to find him anyway.

He didn't need a flashing billboard to see that she how much she cared about him.

And in return, he was hurting her. Over and over again, he was lashing out at her, making sure to let her know that she was nothing but a fuck toy to him.

When the truth was she was anything but.

When the truth was that he didn't want her to

go.

When the truth was that even after only ten minutes together in the cabin, he knew if Janica left, he'd feel the echoes of her everywhere he looked for the next four weeks.

Maybe even for the rest of his life.

The power of these realizations had him reeling.

Her mouth was soft beneath his. Last night their kisses had been rough, caught up in the delirium of their passion. Now, he had the time to learn the curve of her lips, the sweep of her tongue, to find out how much she liked it when he dipped into the corners where her lips met.

Barely pulling back from her mouth, he whispered, "I like you. So much more than you know."

Now she was the one kissing him. "Then take me back to bed, Luke."

He wasn't going to lie, he had enjoyed playing out the dominant-submissive fantasy last night, but those roles weren't who either of them really were. If he could have, he would have told her how sorry he was, but his emotions were still too tangled up, too mangled for the words to come.

He'd have to tell her another way.

He lightly stroked her short, silky hair. "You're beautiful."

"So are you."

The sun was streaming into the cabin's windows as they held each other, and then, she was stepping out of his arms, reaching around to undo the clasp at the back of her bra.

It fell to the ground and he finally got to see her beautiful breasts in the light of day.

He was temporarily paralyzed by his desire for her. A small smile playing on her lips, she hooked her thumbs into the sides of her panties and slowly shimmied them off.

“I'm naked now. Just the way you said you wanted me.”

Was her playful spin on his angry, hard words her way of saying she forgave him? Please, he would give anything to have her forgive him. To have her know that he didn't mean any of the harsh things he'd said. That he wished he could take back all of the harsh things he'd done.

“Now it's your turn,” she said, breaking into his thoughts.

As if it were the most normal thing in the world, she sat down on the couch and crossed her legs, completely naked as she looked up at him and waited for him to comply with her request.

He'd never been with a woman who was so comfortable with her body. With herself, period.

His cock, already hard from their kiss and her striptease, twitched in response to her command. He moved to undo his belt, but she shook her head.

“Shirt off first.”

His entire adult life, Luke had been in control. Whatever he needed, whatever he wanted at the hospital, all he had to do was ask and it was delivered to him. For the first time, it wasn't his show.

Sure, he was bigger, stronger than Janica. He could take over in an instant, pick up her small body and pull her over him. But that wasn't what this was about.

Right now, he needed to not only give her back what he'd taken from her the night before when he'd been completely out of control, he needed to give her the most important thing of all.

His trust.

The question was, could he do it?

Chapter Eleven

There was so much going on in that head of his.

Too much.

"Sex doesn't have to be this complicated, Luke," she said softly.

Wanting to help him, she reached for his hands and pulled him down to his knees in front of her. Wrapping her legs around his waist, she pressed her lips to his forehead, to his cheekbones, to his chin.

Saving the best for last, she pressed her lips to his mouth. All the while, emotion was building up from way down deep in her belly, from the center of her heart, and even though she knew what was coming, even though she knew she shouldn't say it again, she simply couldn't stop herself.

"I love you."

She could feel his breath against her lips, his heart beating against her chest. And then he was kissing her again, and she was pulling off his T-shirt and unzipping his jeans.

His erection was hard and thick and hot against her naked skin.

"Take me, Luke."

In one slow thrust he sheathed himself inside

her and she gasped at how full, how complete she felt. Her pussy lips were still sensitive from their lovemaking the night before, but instead of pain she felt the deepest pleasure she'd ever known. Without even a thin layer of latex between them, she felt truly connected to him.

As connected as he'd let her get.

Luke was sitting back on his shins cradling her body above his. His tongue played with hers, his hands cupped the curve of her ass, the light dusting of hair on his chest tickling her erect nipples as she rocked against him.

Part of her wanted to stay like this forever, but the other part that desperately wanted to ride his hard shaft until they were both crying out in pleasure couldn't be ignored. Using the muscles in her legs, she lifted herself off of his long shaft until only the tip of his head still remained inside, then sank down on him again, as far she could go.

He pulled back from their kiss and captured her gaze.

"Janica."

She couldn't read his expression, apart from the clear desire he felt for her.

She could feel tears coming again. Dammit, why was she crying every single time they had sex? Why couldn't she just concentrate on how good it felt? On the fact that every one of her sexual fantasies about Luke was coming true?

Ducking her head so that he wouldn't see—even though he already knew she loved him and really, what more was there to give to him?—she was surprised to feel the back of his hand beneath her chin tilting her face back up.

"How can you love me?"

His words were a raw whisper. She was surprised by the depth of pain beneath them, by the fact that he didn't seem to know just how wonderful he really was.

Their bodies still entwined in the most elemental of ways, she raised her hands to his face to run her fingertips over his lips, his jaw, his eyebrows. "Well, you're the most beautiful man I've ever seen, for one."

But when he frowned, she knew now wasn't the time for teasing, for easy lines she could feed to any guy.

"I love you because you're good."

Lost in her emotions, she unconsciously shifted her weight on him and as his thick shaft somehow slid in even deeper, on a gasp of pleasure she said, "I love you because you're honest."

Her nerves endings were on fire, not just at the tips of her breasts, not just between her legs, but also the ones inside her chest, where everything she felt for Luke began and ended.

"I love you because you always took care of my sister and I always knew she was safe with you."

The tears were falling now, along with spirals of incredible pleasure which were rippling all across her skin. There was nothing she could do to stop either of them.

"I love you, Luke," she finally whispered in

a voice that shook from the powerful sensations taking her over, body and soul, "because of everything you do and everything you are."

She even loved him despite the fact that she knew he would never love her back, despite the fact that his eyes were dark and unreadable as he listened to her reasons for loving him.

Hating her endless, stupid tears, she fought desperately for control. Wanting to do something, anything to try and guard what was left of her heart, she shifted her weight on his lap to take him deeper.

"And I absolutely love your cock."

The next thing she knew he'd shifted them so that her hips were right at the edge of the couch. Again and again he drove into her, harder and deeper with each thrust. One of his hands fondled her breasts while the other moved to her clit. All it took was the slightest pressure of his thumb on the hard nub between her legs and she was crying out as a shockingly powerful orgasm took her over, one that almost seemed to radiate out from her heart, rather than her pussy.

She heard him say, "You're amazing, sweetheart" as she was coming down from her climax. And although it wasn't even close to the same thing as being in love with her, at least it was something.

At least he'd called her sweetheart.

She could see how tightly clenched his jaw was, how much effort it had cost him not to come with her. She wished he had, wished he had completely lost control, wanted to know that she could do that to him.

He ground out the words, “I need to pull out.”

“No, you don't.” If he left her now, she'd feel so empty. “I'm on the pill. And I'm safe. I swear I'm safe.” Physically at least.

Because the truth was that she'd just put her own heart in the most dangerous position imaginable.

Even for how huge he already was, she felt him grow bigger at her words, thicker, harder.

“Fuck, Janica, I'm gonna come.”

His rough words, said with such heat, sent a new rush of arousal flooding through her. It wasn't going to be the first time she'd had multiple orgasms.

But she was pretty damn sure it was about to be the very best.

“So am I.” She pulled his mouth down to hers and whispered, “Again,” before she kissed him passionately.

And then, he was fucking her fast and hard and she was fucking him right back, their bodies slamming together. Slick skin sliding against slick skin. Mouths biting, sucking. Hands grabbing, pulling. She felt the first shot of his hot ejaculate against the very back of her vagina and she groaned at the extreme pleasure of taking all of him, his very essence, inside of her. Her body reacted with a flood of moisture in the tightening of her inner muscles around his huge shaft, milking him.

Loving him.

* * *

He never wanted to let her go.

Luke started at his unconscious thought. What the hell was he thinking?

Of course he was going to let her go. Just as soon as he'd worked the craziness out of his system, just as soon as he'd had his fill of her heat, her warmth, she'd return back to her normal life. And he'd return to his.

Things would go back to the way they were supposed to be.

The harsh reality of his thoughts made him suddenly realize his knees were killing him on the hardwood floor. Moving slowly – not wanting to let her go, damn it - he maneuvered them both onto the couch, lying back and pulling her body over his like a blanket. Her head settled in at the crook of his shoulder and they lay there together, both catching their breath.

And despite reminding himself that this lapse with his sexy-as-hell sister-in-law was going to have to come to an end in the very near future, over and over, his brain replayed what she'd said.

I love you because you're good.

I love you because you're honest.

I love you, Luke, because of everything you do and everything you are.

The most amazing thing of all was that she could say those things to him when he wasn't being fair to her. When he wasn't being good. Or honest.

LOVE ME *by Bella Andre*

All his life, he'd had a role to play. His brother, Travis, had been the dog. The player. So Luke had taken the opposite side. He'd been the good guy. The honest guy. The safe guy.

It wasn't until last night with Janica that he'd stopped being all those things, that he'd let himself explore the man hiding beneath the layers, beneath the driven surgeon who never let anyone down.

Jesus, he was letting Janica down. He knew he was, with the way he kept using her body, with the way he kept pushing and shoving at her, not just physically, but emotionally.

And still, she thought she loved him.

He still didn't see it. Couldn't possibly understand why. How.

Didn't even begin to comprehend why his chest felt so tight every time she was close. Every time he looked at her, or touched her. Every time she said “I love you.”

He and Janica shouldn't fit together like this. She shouldn't feel like the missing piece of him. Not when anyone could see that the two of them were all wrong for each other.

Completely, impossibly wrong.

But it was hard to think clearly about anything with her naked body warm and soft on his.

He loved the way she smelled, loved the way she tasted, loved the way her taut muscles gave way to purely feminine heat when she was coming.

His muscles that had been so taut since the night before in the ER, except for those few hours when he'd fallen asleep holding her, finally settled down, relaxing into her warmth. He let his eyes drift out to the ocean waves out the front window, seeing how blue it was for the very first time. And then he closed his eyes and unconsciously pulled her closer against him as his mind finally stopped racing.

* * *

Janica felt him fall asleep beneath her, just as he had the night before. She knew how hard he drove himself, knew how exhausted he had to be, and was glad that he felt comfortable enough to fall asleep with her not once, but twice, even with the sunlight streaming in.

She, on the other hand, felt much too amped up to sleep. And she knew if she stayed with him like this, there'd be no way to stop herself from waking him up to make love to him again.

It wasn't that she didn't want to have sex with him again. Of course she did. He was the most spectacular lover she'd ever been with. No one else had ever made her body come alive like he did.

But right now, before she took him inside her body again, before she came apart beneath his mouth and hands, before he pressed his mouth to hers and she took her next breath from his lungs, she needed to figure out a way to deal with all the secrets she'd just admitted to him.

It was one thing to tell him she loved him.

It was another entirely to detail it, to lay it out in such painful clarity.

Now, there was no way she could ever back

away from it. No way she could try to take it back, or say she'd simply been wrapped up in the great sex.

And from this moment forward, her stark emotional admission would always be between them.

Shifting gently out of his arms, she covered him with a blanket, put her clothes back on, and went outside to get her sketchbook out of the car.

During the hardest times in her life, when she felt twisted up inside, the only chance she had of making it through in one piece was if she was putting her feelings down on paper, one image at a time.

So that's what she'd do now, in this cabin on the ocean in Big Sure, with Luke sleeping on the couch beneath a soft blanket she pulled up over his naked body. Even though she already knew that this time the problem was bigger than her pencil and paper.

LOVE ME *by Bella Andre*

Chapter Twelve

Where was she?

Luke kicked off the blanket and sat up, looking for any sign that Janica was still there. But her clothes and her bag were gone.

She was gone.

No!

It was almost impossible to breathe until he walked to the door and saw her sitting on a rock just off the deck, her head bent down over her notepad as she captured the setting sun over the ocean.

My God, she was beautiful. How had he missed seeing her all these years?

Or had he?

His brain spiraled back five years to their meetings about Lily and Travis. Hadn't there been something there? An attraction he hadn't wanted to acknowledge because she was so young, so impetuous, so forward and overtly sexy.

He saw her pencil still on the page, knew she sensed his presence.

Turning her head to look at him, she scanned his naked body with a saucy grin. "It's been a long time since I did a figure model drawing class. You would've caused a riot. For the girls and the boys."

Looking down at himself, he shook his head. He hadn't even realized he was still naked. All he could think about when he woke up was Janica.

If she had left.

Or if she had made the choice to stay.

Closing her notepad, she stood up and said, "I'm starved. Have you got any food?"

"I don't know."

He hadn't been thinking about food when he got here. Just getting drunk.

And feeling sorry for himself.

Moving past him, the soft fabric of her shirt brushing lightly against his already half-mast cock, she went to look in the refrigerator. He had his pants on by the time she pulled out some eggs, a block of cheese, and some sausage.

Watching her maneuver around the kitchen gave him another chance to see her in a completely new light. He'd never thought of her as someone who would even know how to boil water, let alone whip up omelets.

Minutes later, she was pushing a plate over to him. Coming to sit beside him at the kitchen island, she smiled and said, "Sex always makes me hungry," before forking out a bite from the plate.

"This is great." The best omelet he'd ever had. "Where'd you learn to cook?"

"Thanks," she said. And then, "Lily taught me when we were kids." She shrugged. "I guess she figured since we were fending for ourselves she wanted to make sure I never starved if something ever happened to her."

She'd been so young when her parents had died and the Aunt who had taken in Janica and Lily wasn't exactly the motherly type.

"It must've been hard for you."

Again, she shrugged. "Lily took really good care of me. Better than most of my friends' parents."

He knew what she was doing, trying to act tough, like she hadn't been hurt. Because that was just what he'd always done. What he was still doing.

"Still, there's a difference between a sister and a mother. I'm sorry, Janica."

"Don't feel sorry for me. I'm fine."

"Are you?"

Her fork stilled halfway to her mouth. It started shaking in her hand and she dropped it to the plate in obvious frustration.

"Fuck. What is it about you that has me wanting to spill all my secrets?"

He didn't know. But he did know that he wanted to be there for her. For now, at least, while they were spending time together. Later...well, he wasn't going to think about later, didn't want to have to face the aftermath of being so close to Janica. And then not having her in his life anymore.

"Tell me, Janica."

He realized that he hated to see her close herself off to him. That he much preferred the way she looked when she was in his arms and she was totally open, totally pure in her confession of love. Whether or not he believed that her loving him was even possible.

Needing to let her know she could trust him with the pain she felt over losing her paretns at such a young age, he said, “I want to listen to you.”

She stared at him in silence for long enough that he found himself fighting the urge to fidget on the bar stool.

Finally, he saw her come to a decision. To trust him.

“Even when I was a little girl I knew how strong I was. That I'd always figure out a way to take care of myself, no matter what happened. Lily was the emotional one. The soft one. Like I said before, I was so glad that she had you to protect her when we were growing up.” She paused, took a deep breath. A breath that shook a little bit and shifted something inside of his chest, broke something down, a wall he'd built around his heart so long ago. “But the thing is, sometimes my whole tough girl act gets a little old, even for me. Especially when it's what everyone expects from me, all the time.”

He should have been amazed to find out that she wasn't nearly as strong as she seemed. But, then, hadn't he already seen it for himself? When he was making love to her and tears were falling from her eyelashes as she confessed her love, wasn't she just as vulnerable as anyone else?

His voice gentle, he said, “It shouldn't matter what other people expect from you. You should be able to just be yourself.”

She looked out the window at the water,

frowning. "I don't know who else I can be." She turned and gave him a crooked grin that didn't quite reach her eyes. "Take you, for instance. You've always thought I was a total brat."

At this point, he knew better than to try and deny it. She'd know he was lying. And the one thing he knew for sure was that he didn't want to ever lie to her.

"You're right. I did. But that didn't mean I wasn't impressed by you at the same time."

Guilt had already kicked in big time at the way he'd treated her since last night. Before that even. And now that she was being so honest with him, he felt more contrite than ever.

"I don't want to hurt you, Janica."

She blinked at his abrupt statement, her mouth opening slightly, her tongue flicking out in a surprisingly nervous gesture.

"Trust me, I'll tell you if you get too rough." She smiled that sexy smile that sent blood rushing to his groin. "You haven't even gotten close yet."

But he wasn't talking physical. God, he hated having to lay it out like this, but there was no other way. Not if it meant lying to her. Not if it meant making her promises that he couldn't possibly keep.

"Your coming here means more to me than I can say, Janica. But it won't work."

She cocked her head to the side, acting like she didn't know exactly what he was saying.

"It?"

Fuck. She was forcing him to be as brutally

honest as she'd been.

"Us. You and me."

She licked her lips again, dropped her eyes to his mouth. "Seems to me we work together pretty damn well."

Despite the heavy nature of their conversation, his cock instantly responded to her words, to that one look. And the awesome visuals and memories that went with them.

"Look, I've never been more sexually compatible with another woman, but—"

"But this thing we're doing could never be more than sex?"

Shit. He felt like the world's biggest asshole.

"Right," he forced out. Asshole didn't even come close.

She didn't look angry, thank god, but he hated the slight downturn of her beautiful mouth. As if she was tasting something sour.

"Because you're you and I'm me? Apples and oranges?"

Again, he had to force out an, "Exactly."

She stared at him as if daring him to look away. "I don't buy it."

What the fuck? He'd just told her he couldn't foresee any kind of future with her and she was questioning him? Any other woman would've probably been crying. But not Janica.

Despite himself, his respect for her notched up another level.

And a sweet sense of relief that he hadn't seen coming flooded through him as she said, "I think you like me a whole lot more than you want to admit. And don't tell me that if I leave right now you won't be coming by my place later to fuck my brains out again."

A warning light flashed before him. Partly because he was afraid she was right. Partly because he didn't want her to be right. He'd always been in control. Always.

But something told him where Janica was concerned, he might not ever be in control again.

It was unthinkable not to fight it, not to fight what he was feeling, not to fight what he couldn't possibly understand.

"Right there," he said in just as challenging a voice as she'd made her previous statement, "that's exactly why we could never work as a couple."

"A couple, huh?" She cocked one eyebrow up in an exaggerated manner.

She was turning his words around like a lawyer intent on prosecution. "Jesus, Janica, you're not listening to me!"

"Yes I am, Luke."

"No, damn you, you're not!"

Fuck. He never raised his voice. Except with her.

"Actually," she said sweetly, "I thought I'd been listening to you pretty darn well. Did I not drop to my knees or strip fast enough for you last night?"

"And that's another thing," he found himself saying as he tried to keep up with her. "That's not how I have sex."

"Could have fooled me," she retorted. "Seemed like you knew exactly what you were doing." She paused, narrowed her eyes. "At least in my experience."

Jealousy bit him in the ass at the thought of her role-playing with another man. He couldn't stand the vision of another man ripping her dress from her, giving her commands, forcing her to suck his dick.

"How many other guys have you let dominate you?"

"Is that what you did?"

His jaw felt tight from gritting his teeth together so hard. Why couldn't she make this easier on him?

Of course she couldn't. She was Janica Ellis.

The ultimate pain in the ass.

And...the sweetest lover he'd ever had.

"You know damn well what I made you do," he said in rough voice.

She grinned and he was surprised by it. Just as he was continually surprised by everything she did. That was her problem, she was unpredictable. Or, he thought a beat later, maybe the problem was that she was predictably wild. Sexy. Overwhelming to his senses. He just couldn't take her in, couldn't process her in a rational way.

"I loved every single second of 'what you made me do'," she said with finger quotes around the words.

Damn it, she wasn't answering his question. "Tell me, Janica. How many?"

"You're mighty possessive about my sex life, you know, Luke," she said, but he'd already reached—and was headed past—his boiling point.

He shoved their plates across the counter with a loud screech. "Tell me, now, or I swear to God I'm going to—"

Another sexy little smile. "What are you going to do? Spank me?"

Jesus, he shouldn't be getting harder at the thought of spanking her. His palm suddenly itched to caress her ass.

Her eyes widened as she took in his reaction to her teasing. "You actually want to, don't you?"

He shook his head. "I don't."

Fuck.

He did.

"I'm not the submissive type." More softly, "I've never been like that with anyone but you. I've never wanted to be like that with anyone but you."

As she said it, he knew she had to be telling the truth. Because in all the years he'd known her, she'd never been the least bit submissive. It was just that night in her apartment she'd been so perfect, as if she practiced following sexual orders a hundred times.

Unable to understand any of it, he had to ask, "Then why?"

She looked him straight in the eye and said, as if it was the most obvious thing in the world, "Because you needed me."

Chapter Thirteen

There were so many things she wanted to ask him. But there had already been too many revelations on these kitchen bar stools.

"Come on. Let's go outside. Take a walk on the beach before it gets dark."

Without waiting for his agreement, she headed out the door and down the steep set of stairs that led down to the sand. Her body, her brain, felt tingly, jumpy. Like with every word out of her mouth, with every revelation she hadn't intended to reveal, she was changing into someone else.

And suddenly she knew for sure that the woman she'd been last night and the woman she'd be when she left this cabin would be very different people.

Thanks to Luke.

At first she didn't hear his footsteps on the stairs behind her. She was nearly at the bottom before they came.

Clearly, he was having a hard time. With her, obviously. But what else was bothering him so much?

It was exactly what she intended to find out.

Her feet bare, she walked through dry sand

to where it was dark and cold and wet.

For being such a city girl, she had always loved nature. In fact, she rarely worked out in a gym, preferring to go for a hike or an open-water swim.

A wave came in and as the water frothed over her feet, she shivered and wrapped her arms around herself.

"Cold?"

"Come here and feel it for yourself."

When he didn't walk into the surf, she held out an arm to him. "Don't worry, I'll keep you safe."

She realized the hugeness of what she'd said as his eyes bore into her, as serious as she'd ever seen him. She tried to open her mouth to make a joke that would minimize it, but nothing came.

Because she'd meant it. She would keep him safe.

If he would let her.

Finally, he came forward and took her hand. And the incredible thing was, even after all of the amazing things he'd done to her body, his simply holding her hand was the most wonderful thing of all.

Together, they stood at the edge of the surf in perfect silence, holding hands. Janica worked to memorize every sensation. The slightly rough skin of his palm against hers. The smell of salt water and redwood trees. The sun fading behind wispy clouds.

How numb her feet were.

"I can't feel my toes anymore."

She was glad to hear him chuckle. "Me

either."

Not letting go of his hand, she said, "Let's walk some circulation back into them."

Perhaps if she'd been someone else, the perfectly sweet, biddable woman that Luke thought he belonged with, she would have simply been content to enjoy his company out on the sunset beach.

But since there wasn't a chance of that, she said, "Do you like being a doctor?"

His hand tightened on hers at his surprise at her question. "Of course I do."

"What else do you like?"

Another tightening. "There isn't a lot of time for anything else."

Okay, she could see she wasn't going to get very far with this line of questioning. Maybe another tack.

"Why did you become a doctor?"

"What is this? Twenty questions?"

"I just realized that even though we've known each other for so long, we don't know much about each other, do we?"

Except for how perfectly our bodies fit together.

"No," he said slowly, "I don't suppose we do."

But when he didn't answer her previous question, she said, "Was it because of your mom?"

He tried to pull his hand away. But she refused to let him get away that easily. Just as she'd refused to let him say what they were doing could never be more than sex. Even if it was probably the truth when everything was said and done.

Because there was no denying that what went on in the middle of the night in her apartment, what happened between them in the cocoon of a cabin in Big Sur, had absolutely nothing to do with the real world.

But just because it was fact, didn't mean she had to like it.

And it didn't mean she wasn't going to fight it with everything she had.

"When we were back in the cabin, you told me you wanted to listen. I want to do the same for you." When he remained silent, she said, "I never really knew my parents. But you were ten years old when your mom—"

"Dammit, Janica, I don't want to talk about it."

He wrenched his hand out of hers and turned away to head back toward the cabin.

Her heart broke for him, for all the pain he'd kept bottled up inside for so long. And even though she knew she should let him go, leave him alone like he wanted, she simply couldn't walk away from him.

Calling out to him over the waves, she said, "I only have one more question, Luke, and then I promise I'll go."

Thank God, he stopped, turned back to her, his face carved in granite.

"You already know I love you. What else do I need to do to get you to trust me?"

* * *

Jesus. No one but Janica would stand there and ask him that. No one would dare.

Then again, he'd never let anyone in this close. It had never even been a possibility until now.

Until Janica.

They stood there, facing each other in silence long enough that the sun moved completely below the water line.

It wasn't until he could barely make out her face and form in the darkness that he finally admitted, "I don't know." His heart was pounding so hard he could hardly say, "But I do know I don't want you to go."

And then she was moving across the sand into his arms and saying against his lips, "Don't worry. I'm not going anywhere."

Her mouth was soft and sweet. Just like, he was continually surprised to find out, she was.

So sweet.

So soft.

So warm.

"Let's go back upstairs to the cabin so you can fall asleep in my arms again," she whispered, her breath warm against his earlobe.

But when they'd made it back up the stairs, sleep was the last thing on his mind. All he wanted was to be with her again, to lose himself in the comfort and joy of her body.

"I need you," he said, knowing how raw his

statement was, but utterly unable to keep that truth from her.

But there was no victory in her eyes at his admission of need. Just love.

"I know you do. And I need you too."

This time, there was no rush. Neither of them was going anywhere else. And there was no anger, either.

"I want to love you, Janica."

Again she said, "I know you do," and something about the way she responded made him suddenly realize what he'd said. How it sounded.

Like he wasn't just talking about physical lovemaking.

Like he was talking about his heart.

Was he?

The impossible question fell away as she began to strip off his clothes and he reached for hers. Moonlight was streaming in through the windows, illuminating her incredible body.

How could he ever go back from her? How could he ever move on without her? How would another woman ever match up to her?

"I don't know how you're doing it," he found himself saying.

"Doing what?" she asked, her hands continuing to make short work of his clothes.

He tried to figure out how to put it into words, into something that made sense when nothing made sense anymore. "Changing everything." Even the things he hadn't thought needed changing. "So fast."

"You're doing it too, Luke." She reached out and placed her palm flat over his heart. "Changing me. I've never said I love you to anyone else. But with you, I can't seem to stop."

Her words rushed through him, her love pushing up against every wall he'd ever built. It was instinctive for his brain to push back, to tell him to take a step back.

And he would. He had to. For both of their sakes. Because he still believed what he'd said in the kitchen, that the two of them were too different to ever truly be together.

But he couldn't walk away from her now. Not yet. Not when his need was so much stronger than his sense.

It had been exciting to take her on the couch, the living room floor, but right now he needed to love her properly, in a bed.

He scooped her up to take her to the bedroom and she said, "We'll get sand in the sheets."

Looking down at her, wanting her more with every second, he said, "Then I guess we'd better get cleaned up first."

He made a detour into the shower, stepping onto the ocean blue tile with her still in his arms. She reached out and turned the water on, laughing when it came down over them, cold at first, then warmer.

He kissed her, also laughing as the water soaked them, loving how playful she was.

When was the last time he'd been playful at

all? With anyone?

"You know," she said with a wicked little gleam in her eyes, "now that we're here, I think we should make the most of it."

"I completely agree," he said, and then a second later, he was shifting her in his arms so that her legs were around his waist and her arms were around his shoulders. He backed her up against the wall of the shower and kissed her with all the emotion he neither understood, nor could put words to.

He'd taken her so roughly in the living room on the couch with virtually no foreplay. She'd been ready for him then, but this time he swore he was going to take his time with her body. Make sure she had her fill of pleasure before he took his.

But, of course, she had other plans. Because before he could even so much as move his mouth from her lips to her breasts, she was shifting her weight on him, settling her hot pussy lips over the crown of his cock.

"I want to make this good for you," he told her, but she was already sinking down on his cock, taking him in, stretching around him slowly, inch by inch.

"This is good for me. So good."

Knowing he couldn't change her mind even if he wanted to, he gladly went with it, thrusting up into her in the next breath. She took him fully, even though he knew she had to be sore.

"I wanted to be gentle with you this time."

"You are."

He found himself not breathing, not moving, just staring into her eyes. She was staring too and he had a feeling she was seeing down deep into his soul, past the successful surgeon all the way to the real man inside. A man that he wasn't sure he really knew.

"I've never been with anyone like you."

On a little smirk, so cute, so sexy, she replied, "I blow everyone else out of the water, don't I?"

He laughed then, how could he not? She was great.

He'd never liked a woman more.

A point that was only brought home when she said, "Enough with gentle. Fuck my brains out, Luke."

He brought his mouth down hard on hers at the exact moment that he pulled back and thrust deep again. Protecting her head and back from the tile with his hands, together they pounded into each other, driving higher and higher for what they were both wanting.

Needing.

He felt her pubic bone grinding against his, worked like hell to hold himself off until he began to feel her slick inner muscles clench and tighten around his cock. And then he heard her whisper, "I love you so much," and there was no hope left for him but to let his own climax spiral out with hers, wrapped tightly in not only her body, but also her boundless love.

LOVE ME *by Bella Andre*

Chapter Fourteen

Janica woke up in Luke's arms, sunlight streaming in his bedroom window, his lean muscles pressed against hers, his heart beating strong and steady beneath her palm. She shifted against him, loving the play of his body on hers, his hair tickling her smooth skin, the fact that everywhere she was soft, he was hard.

She knew right when he woke up by the way his heart beat faster beneath her hand. She pressed a kiss into his chest before whispering, "Good morning."

His arms tightened around her, and then he was pulling her up his body to kiss her. Just as she had every other time he had pressed his lips to hers, she lost herself in his kiss, gave herself over completely to him, and let down all of her barriers. And then, he was rolling them over so that her back was flat against the mattress and he was levered over her, staring down at her with those sinfully hot eyes of his.

She instinctively opened herself up to him, and he moved right into place, the thick head of his cock pushing against her already wet lower lips. In the next heartbeat he was sheathed completely inside of her and she gasped at the hot, heavy weight of him filling her so perfectly.

Holding himself completely still above her, he continued to stare at her.

"I can't get enough of you."

Again, he wasn't talking about love, and rationally she knew that maybe it would never be anything more than sex for him. But in that moment with her legs wrapped around his hips, her hands gripping his broad shoulders, his heat consuming her, it simply didn't matter.

"Love me, Luke."

His eyes darkened at her words, but before she could take them back or change them or turn them into anything other than what they obviously were, he started moving. His long, hard, ruthless strokes of pleasure inside of her left no room for anything but an all-consuming rush of ecstasy. The feel of Luke's hands and mouth and cock, his murmurs of praise about how beautiful she was, about how good she felt wrapped around him, all came together like an ocean tide that was pulling her deeper into dangerous waters.

She felt herself start to go under a split second before he did, her muscles clenching him so tightly as he pushed even deeper inside her heat.

And all the while, even as she felt him spurt hot and thick into her, even as she cried out his name, his eyes never left hers. It was beautiful, watching him come, the play of pleasure moving across his face, knowing how good she was making him feel.

Minutes later as they lay damp and panting side by side on the bed, he turned his head to her. "You probably need to get back to work in the City, don't you."

"Probably," she agreed.

It was incredibly gratifying to watch disappointment move across his face. And maybe, she thought to herself, even a little mean of her to do that to him. If only to confirm that he'd miss her when she left.

"But I was thinking I could just make some calls instead." She smiled. "I want to stay here with you."

For as long as they could possibly keep the "real" world at bay.

"You don't—"

He cut himself off with a curse and shifted back hard on the bed away from her.

Following her impulse—apparently where Luke was concerned she was unable to do anything else, even when she knew better, even when she knew she was just setting herself up to be destroyed—she moved from her side of the bed and shifted over him so that she was sitting up above him straddling his hips.

"You can say anything to me. You know that, don't you?"

She saw him try to fight a grin and lose the battle.

"Where the hell did you come from?"

Holding her hands out at her sides as if she were trying to fly, perfectly comfortable with her nudity, she said, "I'm one-of-a-kind."

His grin widened, but then, suddenly fell away. "I can't ask you to stay. I shouldn't ask you to stay."

"You use those words too much. Can't. Shouldn't. I think you should stop worrying about a bunch of random rules and get to the real question." She pressed her palms flat against his six-pack, enjoying the feel of his muscles rippling beneath her hands. "What do you want, Luke?"

"I want you to stay."

This time, it was her turn for her grin to fall away at his potent statement. And when he followed it up with, "I don't know what I would do if you left, Janica," she was pretty sure all the breath left her lungs.

Again, it wasn't love, but it was something. Something more than she'd ever thought to hear him say to her, to have him feel for her. Especially considering the way he'd practically been trying to force her out the door before their walk on the beach, when he'd been an apple and she'd been an orange.

But when she looked at him, she could see that there was still something more.

"Say it all, Luke. You don't have to hold back with me."

She could see his brain trying to take over. She moved one hand from his stomach to his heart.

"Keep talking from here, not up there," she said, nodding at his head.

"I just want to be with you. For the next few

days without any—" He cut himself off again. "Fuck, I suck at this, don't I?"

"Kind of," she teased, then decided to let him off the hook by saying, "Are you trying to tell me that you just want to have fun?"

"Fun," he repeated, the word almost hollow. He didn't move or speak again for a long moment. Finally, he said, "That's exactly what I want."

She knew what he was really asking for. No more difficult questions. No more trying to reach inside his heart to uncover everything he kept hidden.

And no more worrying about the real world or either of their opposite places in it.

Her answer was simple. And the only one she could give. Because she wasn't strong enough to leave him. Not when she loved him so damn much it actually hurt.

"Okay."

He didn't look convinced. "I know it's a lot to ask."

Slowly shifting her weight down his hips to get closer to the erection that she'd felt growing against her backside during their conversation, she said, "I'm all for fun," as she wriggled down over him. "Although in the name of full disclosure, there is one thing, though, that I don't think I'm going to be able to promise you."

"Tell me," he said, his hips shifting with hers, easily finding her wet heat.

"I don't think I'm going to be able to stop telling you that I love you."

With that said, she pushed down onto him, taking him all the way to the hilt.

“I don't want you to stop,” he said.

Surprise at his stark admission made her open up even more, both between her legs and behind her breast-bone. “I won't, Luke. No matter what.”

But in the aftermath of their orgasms, Janica realized she didn't actually know what he'd meant. Had he simply been telling her not to stop the erotic slide of her body against his because he'd been about to come?

Or was it the outpouring of love from her heart that he didn't want to end?

Chapter Fifteen

Luke couldn't remember feeling like this since he was a little boy. When he was with Janica, he caught snippets of freedom. Of happiness.

And the sex was beyond great.

Jesus, he'd never come like this, not with anyone else. He finally understood why the French called it "la petite mort." Being with Janica, taking her to the edge and then following her over, almost felt like it was obliterating the dark patches inside of him, one orgasm at a time.

The next day when they could finally stop devouring each other's bodies, they drove a couple miles down the road to go for a hike and then she made him stop at every little store and cafe on the way back to the cabin. What should have taken fifteen minutes, took over an hour. He'd never met anyone as interested in everything around her. Especially when he knew that, if it were up to him, he would have kept his focus on the unimportant goal of getting back to the cabin to the exclusion of all else.

In the afternoon, she apologized about having to take care of some work. He knew she was successful, but he hadn't realized quite what an extensive operation she ran until he caught snippets of her detailed conversations from the kitchen over the next few hours.

Two days with her and he couldn't imagine what that kitchen would look like without her in it. He couldn't imagine sleeping alone. Hell, he couldn't even imagine showering alone at this point.

He hadn't invited her to come here, to invade his life, but now that she was here the crazy truth was that he was glad.

So damn glad it scared the shit out of him.

Because he knew it couldn't possibly last forever, this fantasy world they were living in just steps away from the ocean and the forest.

It was getting dark when he realized he was missing her too much to stay outside and give her privacy any longer. She dropped the phone on to the counter just as he walked in, looking mildly irritated.

And totally beautiful.

He knew another moment of fear. It was a big deal for her to give him these days away from her business. The look on her face after hanging up the phone told him how badly she was needed at the office.

She was going to leave.

No. Not yet!

His entire body tensed. His gut clenched tight, like it was being held by a ruthless fist. He needed to stop her, had to convince her somehow, someway, to stay. At least for a little while longer.

Because he needed her. So badly it shocked

the hell out of him.

She swept out of the cabin. "I need to go dancing. Now."

She threw his car keys at him and he barely caught them before they fell over the edge into the thick brush. "You're not leaving?"

The words came out before he could stop them, before he could delete the pathetic undertone of need, of fear beneath them. She stopped running down the stairs to look back at him with a frown.

"Not without you, I'm not."

The rush of relief, of joy, nearly knocked him over.

By the time he got down to the bottom of the stairs she was standing in the gravel parking lot looking disapprovingly at his Porsche. Every other woman he'd ever been with had practically wanted to do his car.

Somehow it was fitting that Janica seemed annoyed by it instead.

"Why can't you just drive a truck?" Before he could answer, she shot him an irritated glance, and said, "Because let me tell you, it's going to be hell trying to do it in this stupid sports car."

He laughed out loud and got hard all at the same time. "I thought we were going to go dancing?"

She rolled her eyes. "Dancing. Fucking. One leads right to the other. How can you not know that?" She opened the passenger door, got in, and slammed the door.

He was going to have a hell of a time

dancing with a hard-on like this. Not that it really mattered, however, since he didn't dance. In any case, he seriously doubted they'd find a place to dance in this fairly remote coastal mountain town.

Which meant they could just focus on the fucking, he thought with a grin that he had a feeling he was going to pay for later.

But maybe she was a little witch. Because they had barely hit the two lanes of Highway 1 when she had him pull over in front of a biker bar. The parking lot was packed with motorcycles and big trucks.

He could hear the music blaring before he'd even turned off his ignition.

Still in the front seat of his car, she turned and looked at him with a wicked gleam in her eyes. "You are going to absolutely hate this, aren't you?"

"Fuck, yes."

She threw her head back and laughed, then got of the car and all but skipped inside the bar.

Wondering why he was even bothering to lock his car in a place like this – it would only be more fun to steal if it was a challenge, wouldn't it? - he headed inside after her. She was already in the middle of the dance floor by the time he got inside, shaking and shimmying and writhing with everything she had.

Quickly noting he wasn't the only one drinking her in, knowing without a shred of doubt that every guy in there—and probably half the women—wanted to drag her into a back room and take her, a swift burst of red-hot jealousy rushed him. Without thinking, he pushed through the crowd to lay claim to her.

As if she'd expected him to do just that, she spun into his arms and wrapped them around his neck, pulling his mouth down to hers.

If there was a better feeling than claiming Janica like this, he sure as hell didn't know what it was. Something took him over then, a feeling of deep release. Similar to how he felt when he was pouring himself into her body, but different at the same time. It was the most natural thing in the world to dance with her there in the middle of a biker bar to country songs about drinking too much and sleeping with the wrong guy.

Maybe it was the way her eyes shined as she looked at him.

Or maybe it was just how right it was to be with her, doing anything.

Anything at all.

Song after song they danced, Janica moving in and out of his arms, her hips brushing and swaying against his, her breasts slipping and sliding against his chest, his arms, his hands, until he couldn't take it anymore. Because she was right, dancing and fucking were practically the same thing, only he couldn't take her in a crowded bar in front of a roomful of strangers.

Without a word, he grabbed her hand and pulled her off the dance floor, past the bar, and out to his car. Only taking the time to open his door, he practically threw her across the car onto her seat.

He could scent her as he peeled out of the

parking lot, her sweet smell of heat and arousal and pleasure completely obliterating any remnants of the beer and smoke that had surrounded them inside the bar. Neither of them spoke, not even her, and barely a minute later he was pulling off the road onto a dirt track that led to a beach trail. In the thick of the woods, he yanked his keys out of his car, shoved his seat back as far as it would go, and grabbed her out of her seat by her hips, pulling her on top of him.

"You make me crazy," he said, and then his lips were on hers and he was ripping at the thin straps of her dress, pulling them down past her breasts. She shifted up on him and he sucked one hard, pink nipple into his mouth, swirling around it with his tongue before taking it between his teeth.

She ground herself into him, begging him without words to give her the release they both desperately needed. It didn't matter that he'd made love to her twice that morning.

He needed her again.

Now.

Cupping her breast to his mouth with one hand, he shifted his lips to her nipple, tasting, sucking, devouring. His free hand slipped under the short skirt of her dress to cup her mound, damp and sizzling hot beneath his palm.

"I've got to touch you," he said against her skin, and then he was sliding one finger into the leg band of her silk panties and sweeping it through the slick moisture that coated her labia.

She thrust down on his fingers and he added

one more, then another until she was practically sobbing and holding his head against her breasts. Shifting his hand just slightly, he rubbed his thumb against her clit with every ramming stroke of his fingers inside her heat.

“Luke,” she moaned. “Yes, please, there, oh God.”

She went perfectly still for a split second as the pleasure hit her and then she was moving again, even faster, her pussy drawing on his fingers, her clit slamming against his thumb, her muscles wrapping themselves around him tighter and tighter as she exploded.

But even as she came, he could feel her fingers working on the button at the top of his jeans.

“Next time you come you're not going to be able to do another goddamned thing,” he growled as she pulled open his pants and reached for his cock.

Her eyes opened then, and she looked at him in beautifully unfocused pleasure. “I need to have you in me.”

He had to kiss her, had to take her, had to be with her, inside her, in every possible way. His tongue found hers just as his cock began to slide into her tight, wet canal. She was tighter than she'd ever been, even that first night, and somewhere in the only part of his brain that could still hold thought, he knew he was being way too rough with her, taking her too many times, too fast, too hard.

Fighting for control, he gripped her hips, stopping them with only his head inside her pussy lips.

"We need to go slower, sweetheart."

"No," she said, clearly trying to use every bit of strength she possessed to force herself out of his grip and slide down onto his cock.

But he'd made up his mind. For her sake, even though it was probably going to kill him, they had to take their time.

"It'll be even better this way," he said, working like hell to convince not only her, but himself, as he said it. "One inch at a time."

To illustrate his point, he moved her body down over him just enough to cover that inch.

A thick rush of moisture immediately coated his cock and she sucked in a breath.

"I love it when you boss me around," she said in a breathy voice with a sexy little grin.

Through the thick haze of his lust for her, he managed a grin. "And I love it when you obey."

"Only you," she whispered in response. "I only want to obey you, Luke."

He throbbed thick and strong inside of her, his cock only growing bigger and harder and more demanding the more control he tried to exert over it. He had to get in deeper, had to take another inch of her sweet, slick heat. As he shifted her yet again he could feel her opening up around him, her aroused and swollen flesh both giving to him and taking from him in equal measure.

And then she was saying, "Oh my God, I'm going to come again," in a low, raw voice.

He could hardly believe it, that without anything more than not quite half of his cock inside her, her muscles were tightening down on him, squeezing his sensitive cock head for everything it was worth. Whatever shreds of control he had left were immediately lost as he pulled her mouth down to his and ravaged her with his lips and teeth and tongue. In the next breath his cock was in to the hilt and he was right there with her as she cried out into his mouth, his groans of pleasure indistinguishable from hers.

Chapter Sixteen

The next day they went for a long walk on the beach and Janica filled up his pockets with seashells, exclaiming that each one was "the most beautiful one she'd ever seen." They bought some clams and mussels out on the pier and had the messiest lunch in memory feeding each other buttery mollusks, which only got messier when Janica stopped eating and instead squirted them at him, shooting them out of their shells like little slippery missiles. His immediate thoughts about the huge mess they were making and what a pain in the ass it was going to be to clean up were quickly overridden by the need to nail her with his own uneaten clams.

They'd ended up fully dressed in the shower, cleaning each other carefully, first with a bar of soap and their hands, and then their mouths, and then he took her up against the tile wall again. It had been a combination of playful and hot and hungry too that he'd never known existed.

Night fell and they made burgers on the grill, also polishing off a bag of potato chips. Luke could have easily written a textbook on proper nutrition, but it was the strangest thing that instead of having less energy after easing up on the "good" stuff, he had more.

But it wasn't the food, he knew.

It was Janica.

As his mid-30s had crept up on him he'd been more and more careful about diet and exercise. But with her he felt at least a decade younger. Still, when she reached into the grocery bags after dinner and pulled out a huge bag of marshmallows and chocolate and graham crackers, he decided that next time he should pay closer attention to what they bought at the store.

Of course, that would mean he'd somehow have to learn how to stop focusing on her ass as she walked down the aisles.

Which meant that it was far more likely he'd have to get used to eating crap food. Because her ass was a goddamned miracle.

It wasn't until he was almost past his thoughts, that he realized where he was going with them. *When had grocery shopping with Janica in the future become something that was a given beyond the next few days?*

He knew better, knew he'd been horribly remiss about stopping things between them from going any further. Where Janica was concerned, right now he just didn't have it in him to be the strong one. To be the voice of reason. To do the right thing, no matter the personal cost.

He looked up just as she threw the bag of marshmallows at him, and then the chocolate. He caught them right before they nailed him in the forehead.

After grabbing a box of graham crackers, she headed for the door. "How are your fire-making skills?"

He nailed her with a hard look that told her she didn't know who she was messing with. "I was the top scout in my troop."

"Of course you were," she teased. "I don't know why I even bothered to ask. Some things are just a given, aren't they?"

"Hey," he said as he caught up to her and grabbed her around the waist, "don't knock the outdoor skills, babe. Hands down, there's no one you would rather be lost in the woods with."

She reached her hand up to his cheek. "Even without the mad scouting skills, there's no one I would rather be with. In the woods or otherwise." And then she pulled out of his hold and scampered down the stairs.

His head, his heart, reeled as he followed after her.

She'd held up her end of the "just fun" bargain really well so far. Almost too well. So far, that had been her only slip.

But knowing how much she enjoyed being with him wasn't what had him reeling. After all, he already knew she loved him.

No, what gave him pause was how much he liked hearing her say it.

How much he liked knowing it.

Too damn much.

She was already collecting rocks and

arranging them in a circle on the sand by the time he reached her with an armful of sticks and broken logs that he'd found in the woods between the cabin and the beach. It was a still night out on the coast, and he easily lit a match and put it to the kindling. Minutes later, a bonfire was roaring.

It was the most natural thing in the world to sit down on a blanket in front of the fire with Janica between his legs, her back pressed to his stomach, his arms around her, holding her tight. They stared into the flames in silence for quite a while, her head leaning back against his chest, his chin resting lightly on the top of her dark head.

But despite what should have been the perfect peace of being out on the beach under the stars, Luke felt as if his insides were shifting around, conflicting emotions pushing at each other inside his chest.

He wanted to know more about this beautiful woman he was holding. He already knew just how she like to be kissed, stroked. He knew what made her cry out with pleasure, exactly how to take her to the peak and over.

It wasn't enough, damn it.

"Did you always know you wanted to design clothes?"

He felt the slightest tightening of her body against his before she replied. "Pretty much. Lily used to take me to the store and buy whatever dolls were on sale."

"What kind of doll goes on sale?"

He loved feeling her laughter rumble

through her chest to his. "The really ugly ones. But they weren't ugly for long, because we'd head to the fabric store next and rifle through their scrap bins. You could fill a bag for five dollars. I'd spend hours cutting and sewing at home."

"Why do I have a feeling you weren't making your dolls pretty little dresses?"

He felt the light jab of her elbow against his ribs. "Are you accusing me of making them look like little Goth sluts?"

He brushed the hair away from the side of her neck and pressed a kiss there by way of an apology. "No. But you definitely don't look at things the way everyone else does."

Her skin was so soft, so sweet smelling, one kiss wasn't enough.

He wanted more.

And not just more of her incredible body. He wanted more of her. More information about what made her tick. More stories about how she'd grown from a little girl into this incredible woman.

"Was it hard to start a business?"

She shifted again in obvious surprise at his question and her hair shifted back to cover her neck. "I thought we weren't asking questions?"

She was right. He'd asked for fun. And nothing but. If he were being smart, he'd simply strip her clothes off and make love to her, no more words, no more getting inside her head. Her heart.

But it wasn't enough.

"I want to know more about you."

The silence stretched out between them, the

crackling of the fire and the waves washing up on the shore not nearly big enough to fill it.

Finally, she softly said, “I was a little scared.”

It took him a long moment to realize she was answering his earlier question, rather than commenting on his wanting to know her. Because she had to know, just as he did, that it was a really bad idea to talk like this, to get in even deeper with each other.

“But even though I was scared,” she continued, “I knew I would regret it forever if I didn't go for what I wanted.”

He wasn't ready for the way her words settled themselves way down deep in his gut and was glad when she didn't let them linger.

“I have Lily to thank for so much of my success. I can't even calculate how many hours she sat there on the floor and clapped and cheered while my dolls gave imaginary fashion shows. And she was such a sensation in my final show for school, and then my first show on my own.”

“I love Lily too,” he said, “but I'm not asking about her. I'm asking about you.”

“Well, here's something you should know about me.” She moved out of his arms and reached for a stick and the bag of marshmallows. “I have a major sweet tooth.”

He shouldn't be feeling disappointed at her clear switch away from his probing. He should be thanking her for keeping them in safe territory.

Fuck. Who was he kidding? They hadn't

been anywhere near safe territory since the moment he rang her doorbell and kissed her.

She handed him a long stick and a couple of marshmallows and side by side they held them over the flames. A minute later they were assembling their s'mores. The sound she made when the sugar and chocolate hit her tongue was almost enough to make him jealous.

"That good, huh?"

She opened her eyes back up and smiled at him. "Only one thing is better."

She pressed her lips against his and he tasted the lingering sweetness on her tongue.

"What about you?" she whispered against his lips.

What was it about kissing her that made him lose hold of his brain, he wondered as he repeated, "Me?"

"Do you like it?"

"I love kissing you."

She pressed her lips back to his, harder this time. When she pulled away, she said, "Good. But I was talking about your dessert."

He looked at the s'more in his hand as if it was the first time he'd seen it.

"Take a bite," she insisted.

Food had never been all that important to him before, simply something he took care of to keep his energy up. And it had certainly never been sensual.

Until now.

Her eyes never left his mouth as he bit into

the gooey treat. He felt crumbs on his lips but he didn't have time to brush them away, because Janica's tongue made it there first.

He barely managed to swallow as she sat back, waiting expectantly for his answer.

"So?"

"It's good. But I still like the taste of your kisses better."

Her smile was as bright as the bonfire. "You know, with lines like that you could have given your brother a run for his money."

Knowing she and Travis had always had a fairly bumpy relationship, he said, "He's a good guy. Better than most people know."

She looked uncharacteristically serious. "I see the way he treats Lily. I know how good he is. But that doesn't change his past."

Something about her statement, something about the words, But that doesn't change his past, sent a warning bell clanging through his head. He ignored it, though, because he was far more concerned with wanting to see another smile on her face than any more warning signs. Lord knew, there'd been a bucket full of them thrown at him since their first kiss. And he'd ignored them all.

"You may find this hard to believe," he told her, "but when we were kids, I was the daredevil."

She cocked her head, looked at him. "I'm not that surprised, actually. You do have a sort of latent wild look about you," she teased.

"If you're not careful I'm going to shove the rest of that s'more into your mouth just to keep you quiet."

"I can think of something else you could shove into my mouth to keep me quiet," she offered wickedly.

"Don't tempt me," he growled, pulling her back against his chest. And, of course, he wanted to feel her taking his cock into her mouth. Who wouldn't?

The thing was, right now he wanted to talk to her even more.

You're asking for trouble, a voice in the back of his head that had joined the warning bell cautioned him, but then she was saying, "Tell me more about all the trouble you got Travis in."

"I learned to swim before he did, which he hated because he always liked to think of himself as the older brother. Those sixty seconds before I came out are really important to him, you know."

"Figures," she said.

Laughing, he said, "Anyway, one afternoon when he was being a real piece of work, we were out by the pool and I dared him to jump into the deep end."

"The idiot jumped, didn't he?"

Luke laughed too, remembering. "Of course he did. But in the end, it all worked out just fine for him."

"Why? Because you saved him?"

"Yeah, I saved him. But it was our busty young babysitter who made his day. I swear he sat there with his head between her breasts the rest of the afternoon."

"How old were you?"

"Six. Seven, maybe."

Janica giggled. "Come on. He was just a kid. He couldn't have already been such a dog. Now you're just talking smack about him because you know I like to hear it." And then she said, "But I'll admit, it was pretty weird when he started dating my sister. I guess I always thought that she'd end up with you."

"No chance," he said. "Lily and I were only friends."

"But you spent so much time together. How could nothing have happened? Something had to have happened at some point."

Fuck. This was awkward.

"We kissed once," he admitted.

"Aha! I knew it."

"We had zero chemistry, Janica."

"How could someone have zero chemistry with you?"

He had to kiss her. "I'm flattered."

"Flattery has nothing to do with it, Luke." She ran the pad of her thumb across his lips. "You're the best kisser I've ever known."

He leaned in to capture her sugary lips and it was the sweetest kiss they'd ever shared.

"I love you," she whispered against his lips.

The three words ricocheted through him just as they always did. And each time something inside of him shifted a little bit more.

Allowing himself one more sensuous sweep of his tongue against hers, he pulled back. "Janica, I

—"

Her eyes were dilated, her cheeks so flushed with arousal that he could see the heightened color on her face even in the dim firelight.

"Shut up and kiss me some more, Luke."

Every time she gave him an out.

And every time he deserved it less.

But the worst part of it was that he knew he was going to take it anyway.

His mouth never leaving hers, he laid her back on the blanket. He wanted to look at her, this beautiful miracle in his arms. Shifting so that he could run his hands over her shoulders, slowly down her arms, he drank in the sight of her.

Firelight made her skin glow, but she didn't need it, didn't need anything other than the fire that was already inside of her.

"I'm so damn lucky you're here." His statement was out there before he could think better of saying it.

She blinked up at him, her big brown eyes warm with arousal—and love. "You are?"

Her response took him by surprise, the fact that she didn't know it already.

And it made him want her even more. It made him want to show her how lucky he was, rather than just tell her with words.

The surf crashed around them as he slowly stripped off her clothes. The moon shined down over them as he ran kisses over her skin. The fire flickered as she cried out with pleasure in his arms.

As he made love to Janica Ellis, the warning

bells and lights clanged and chimed and shined as loudly as they could, trying to remind him that the higher the heights, the bigger the fall. But with Janica moving beneath him and the stars up above in a cloudless sky, he couldn't stop himself from feeling greater pleasure—and deeper peace—than he ever had before.

Chapter Seventeen

"Go back to sleep," Janica murmured as she felt Luke shift against her the following morning.

In the past few days she'd learned that her lover was an early bird. No matter how late they went to bed, no matter how little sleep they got, he was up with the sun.

The only thing that made it slightly palatable was the fact that other parts of him were up too.

"I'll let you sleep again soon," he said, but she was already shifting her hips against his.

Her pussy was deliciously sensitive as he moved into her. She gasped at the wonderful feeling of fullness and he stilled behind her.

She knew he was worried that he was hurting her. His concern was so sweet.

And so misplaced.

"Don't hold back." When he still didn't move, she actually found herself begging him. "Please, Luke. Please."

And then his hand gripped her raised hipbone hard, his fingers digging into her skin right before he thrust into her so deep, so fast that his weight would have pushed her off the bed if he hadn't been holding her steady.

"More," she pleaded. "Give me more."

A second later he had her on her stomach, gripping the sheets with clenched hands as he drove into her from behind. She took everything he had to give and her body silently begged for more as she lifted her hips up off the bed for even deeper penetration.

"Jesus, Janica," he groaned and she was almost too far gone to feel his teeth sink into the curve of her neck as they both exploded with pleasure.

She loved it, loved knowing that she was the only one who could make him lose control like this. She fell back asleep with a smile on her lips.

She wasn't surprised that his side of the bed was empty when she finally woke up. After a shower she walked out of the kitchen to make herself something to eat and found a note on the counter.

"Heading out for a run. Hoping I still have the energy."

She smiled at the note and enjoyed the thought of seeing him return sweaty and out of breath. It was one of her favorite looks on him.

But as she grabbed a banana off of the counter and peeled it, her smile fell away. Making love on the beach in front of the fire with Luke had been way beyond her wildest fantasies. She'd felt special. No other man had ever made her feel like that.

And yet...

She couldn't stop thinking about their

conversation about Lily and Travis and how they'd found true love together. Their siblings were the last two people on earth that should have ended up blissfully happy together. Instead, they had disproved every cynic.

More than once during the past five years, Janica had been, well, not jealous, exactly. But wanting. Wanting what her older sister had. Wanting someone who would walk through flames for her.

Could Luke ever be that person?

Could Luke ever love her? If they left Big Sur and went back to San Francisco, back to their lives, was there any way they could still be together? Or would she forever exist for him in this little cabin by the beach, and only there?

She put the banana down without taking a bite.

She rewound through the past three days and nights, through laughter and loving. And uncertainty, too. Because they were wading through deep, confusing waters together.

After they'd made love out on the beach, when they'd gotten chilly lying naked in each other's arms with only the corners of the blanket to pull up around them, they'd gathered up their things and Luke had gotten a bucket and poured sea water over the bonfire.

Fear had hit her, a punch straight to the solar plexus, as she watched the beautiful flames smolder, smoke, and then sizzle away to nothing.

Please, she'd silently prayed up to the stars in the dark night sky above*, don't let that happen to* *us.*

This wasn't like her, sitting around worrying, acting scared. It also wasn't like her to neglect her business, so she picked up the phone on the counter and checked her messages. If it were anyone but Luke, she would head straight back and not leave her office for a week.

But she couldn't even think of leaving him. He was too important. And he still needed her. The demons he'd been fighting that first night in her apartment were still there, just pushed into the background.

Besides, wasn't that supposed to be one of the perks of having her own business? That she could walk away from it and trust her excellent employees to take care of things if she really needed to?

Fortunately, today there was nothing too pressing for her to deal with. Just a friend in the business who was wondering if she knew anyone who could fill in as a volunteer for "A Day in The Life of a Fashion Designer" at a teen center in Monterey.

She was just finishing up her conversation with him, saying, "No. It's no problem. I'll be there soon," when Luke walked in the door.

"You're leaving."

This was the second time he'd assumed she was halfway out the door. And both times he'd looked pretty darn devastated.

Interesting....

It shouldn't have made her so happy to see

how upset he was. But it did. Which was why she let him hang there for a little while longer with a simple, "Yup."

His jaw tightened, a muscle jumping in the hollow beneath his cheekbone. "This morning. I shouldn't have—"

She took pity on him. How could she not?

"Oh yes you should have," she said with a smile. "In fact I'd be begging you to do the exact same thing to me again right now if we weren't going to be late."

"What are we late for?"

He was clearly confused, but just as clearly relieved that she wasn't leaving.

Laughing, she said, "We've got a hot date with a teen center in Monterey. You'd better get yourself into the shower before I drag you there myself."

But when he held out a hand to her and said, "We'd better get clean, then," even though she knew they were barely going to make it to the teen center on time, she couldn't resist joining him.

* * *

Janica was fantastic with kids.

She was fantastic with everyone, actually. In the first half hour she'd managed to teach Luke enough for him to work with the kids one-on-one as they cut and stitched fabric.

Hours later as they ate clam chowder out of bread bowls at a restaurant on the wharf, he said,

"Looks like you've done a lot of volunteering with kids. I'm really impressed."

"Right back at you," she said. "I don't think any of them knew you were really a stuffy doctor."

He knew he hadn't caught his hurt reaction in time by the way she looked at him and the fact that she covered his hand with hers.

"Sorry, I was just teasing. I really appreciate you helping out today. I know it's a lot of work. If you're ever looking to get out of the ER, you should consider being a pediatrician."

"I loved working with the kids, teaching them what you were teaching me, too." And he had, but that wasn't the full truth. "What I really loved was being with you."

"You loved being with me," she repeated in a hollow voice. "Is that it?"

He frowned, his frown deepening as her face lost all color. God, he hated doing this to her. Especially when he'd known all along that he couldn't give her what she wanted.

"Janica." Fuck. He didn't have the first clue what to say to her.

Because he didn't have the first clue about what was going on inside his own screwed up head.

"I need to get some air," she said, pushing away from the table.

She was fast enough that he couldn't catch her until she was halfway down a public dock. She didn't stop when he called out her name several times and he had no choice but to grab her arm and force her to look at him.

"What's wrong?"

"Me. I'm what's wrong."

"No. You're perfect."

"Then why don't you love me?"

He crushed her mouth beneath his without thinking. He kissed her savagely, ruthlessly. They were both panting when he finally drew away from her bruised and swollen lips.

"I'm hurting you," he said, the words low and raw. "Just like I knew I would. I don't want to hurt you, sweetheart."

"I know you don't," she said, and then she surprised him by taking his hand and saying, "Let's go back to the cabin and you can make it up to me."

He didn't deserve her. Didn't deserve how open and loving she was.

And yet, even knowing that, even knowing he was hurting her, wasn't enough to make him give her up.

Chapter Eighteen

She felt nervous. God, how she hated feeling nervous. They hadn't said a word to each other the whole drive back home. And now they were standing in the cabin staring at each other, like two strangers who didn't know how or where to start. It didn't matter that they knew each other's bodies intimately. Somewhere along the way, their relationship had changed from being purely physical.

Moving straight into the gray area.

A gray area where it felt like her heart might break at any moment.

Where there was more than a slight chance that it already had.

"This shouldn't be so complicated," she said, forcing herself to reach for the zipper on the front of her dress and pull it down, just as she would with any other guy she wanted to sleep with. "I'm a girl and you're a boy and we want each other."

But even as she said the words she knew it wasn't Luke she was trying to convince.

She was trying to convince herself.

"Janica, stop."

Her fingers stilled on her zipper. He moved

across the room, his eyes dark with desire and something else that she couldn't read. And then the next thing she knew he was lifting her in his arms and walking back to the bedroom. Gently, so gently she could hardly believe it, he laid her down on the bed.

She felt like her heart was going to pound out of her chest.

"You don't have to do this." But he didn't stop the slow shift of her dress off of her shoulders, not even when she added, "Please don't do this just because of what I said on the wharf."

His mouth was hot on her shoulder, his lips teasing her skin, and then he was shifting her dress down further, down over her breasts, past her nipples. The pads of his thumbs brushed over her first, followed by his tongue, swirling, tasting.

His sweet touch felt so good she lost her breath.

A while later he lifted his head from her chest. "What were you saying?"

She looked up into his eyes and she was surprised to see the playful glint in the green depths. But, for the first time in a very long time, she didn't want to laugh away her feelings.

"You don't have anything to make up to me, Luke. It's been my decision to be with you. Because I want to."

The sentence was barely out of her mouth before his mouth was back on her breasts, hot and demanding. From one to the other he nipped, kissed, sucked, until she was nearly delirious with pleasure.

Finally, he looked up at her again. “Anything else?”

What had she been about to say? Lust, arousal had her brain all fogged up.

Still, she managed, “It's okay if it's just sex.”

It wasn't. Not at all. But she felt she needed to say it. That maybe then she might be able to believe it.

His hands were gentle, but her dress was still gone by the time she blinked, her panties going a moment later. Moving down between her thighs, he lifted her legs up, one over each shoulder. Her body wept with need for this complex, beautiful man between her legs.

A muscle jumped in his jaw and his eyes were dark. “This isn't just sex.”

She barely had time to process his words when he ran his tongue over her in one long, steady stroke across her labia and over her clit.

Her hips bucked up into his mouth and he held her closer with his hands on her ass, sucking her in between his tongue and the roof of his mouth. Just like that, she came, exploding into him. Spasms of ecstasy racked her body, and it was too much, too much pleasure. But when she tried to shift away, he wouldn't let her go, wouldn't let her escape the almost painful pleasure of his tongue, his lips, the slight scratch of his teeth against her incredibly aroused flesh.

Again she came, hard on the heels of her first orgasm, and she was so lost in feeling, so utterly unable to do anything but try to withstand the waves of pleasure that were rolling over her, that she was caught utterly unaware by the long, hard thrust of Luke's cock inside her.

Her eyes shot open to find him levered over her, his eyes dangerous as he held himself deep inside of her.

She held her breath. Waiting as he continued to watch her, his hard shaft pulsing inside her body, his muscles taut above hers. Waiting for whatever it was he needed to say.

"Luke?"

"I'm almost there," he said softly, and then he started to move, the long slide of his cock out of her slick heat, then back in, so deep that she lost her breath with every single stroke.

And yet, even as she climbed higher and higher, even as her muscles tightened on him, even as their mouths found each other and they swallowed each other's groans of pleasure, even as he pulled her into his arms and exhaustion swept over her and she started to fall asleep, she wondered what he really meant by *I'm almost there*.

Had he been trying to say that he was almost in love with her?

Or was it simply his body that couldn't get enough?

Chapter Nineteen

The next morning, Janica still felt unsettled from their lovemaking.

It was always incredible and explosive between them. But last night was different.

Almost as if Luke's body was trying to express love where the man who lived in it couldn't.

Waking up alone beneath the thick bedspread, she could smell breakfast wafting in from the kitchen. Her muscles were achy, well used and stretched out in a really good way. It sure beat the hell out of running on a treadmill.

Five minutes later she was freshly showered and wearing one of Luke's T-shirts with nothing else under it. Fresh out of clean clothes, she had grabbed one of his belts and wrapped it twice around her waist to finish off the outfit.

He sensed her before she said a word, his eyes drinking her in.

"Nice outfit."

Her nipples beaded at his slow perusal of her outfit. But the truth was she was freaked out enough by what had happened between them then night before that she had to force a playful response.

"You should see what I have on under your

shirt."

She moved to him and he ran his hands down her back, past the belt, then over the curve of her ass.

"You don't have anything on under it," he growled into her ear. He nipped at her neck. "We need to get you some clothes today."

"I thought you liked me just like this?"

"I do. But no one else gets to see what's mine." He pulled back, held her gaze. "You're all mine, Janica."

After last night, after the way he'd told her he was almost there, was this his way of asking her to be his girlfriend?

Torn between outright asking him and the promise she'd made to drop everything but having a good time for the next few days, she was trying to figure out what to say when the front door flung open.

Lily stood there, red-faced and panting as if she'd just run up the long staircase to the cabin. At first, relief was clear on her face. But it was quickly superseded by a strange combination of happiness and shock and dismay.

Luke's arms were instantly frozen around Janica, his muscles turning to ice against hers. His expression quickly followed suit.

Sixty seconds earlier, he'd been so open, so warm. Now he looked – and felt - as closed off as she'd ever seen him.

She wanted to rewind to yesterday so that she could call Lily and tell her she was all right. So that Lily wouldn't have to come here.

And accidentally ruin everything.

"Thank God you're here, Janica," Lily said, holding one hand over her heart, still standing in the doorway. "I've called you a hundred times. And when I went by your studio, your employees said they didn't know where you were. They said you've been calling to check in with them, not the other way around."

Janica hated feeling like a recalcitrant child. She hated that her sister had been worrying about her. But most of all she hated that she hadn't proactively dealt with the situation.

"I'm fine, Lils," she said, but even to her own ears, her voice sounded funny. Like she couldn't take in enough oxygen.

Luke's arms dropped from her waist and although she hadn't noticed him taking any steps away from her, suddenly there was distance between them.

A huge gap that hadn't been there five minutes ago

Suddenly she remember how it had been for them five years ago. They'd met several times to talk about Lily and Travis's budding relationship, they'd even flown to Italy together, just in time for the surprise wedding. She'd thought then that they were starting to build a connection, but as soon as they got back to San Francisco, back to the "real" world, Luke had changed back into the busy surgeon who couldn't be bothered with his wild sister-in-law. Even at family events his smile had gone from warm to cold, to treating her like she wasn't the least bit special.

Oh god. Even after everything they'd shared together - not just the lovemaking, but the little pieces of her heart that she'd so willingly given to him – he was going to do it again.

Looking at him, frozen and stiff as he continued to back away from her in the kitchen, Janica had never been more sure of anything in her life.

Her chest squeezed. She knew she needed to deal with Lily, but she couldn't pull her eyes from Luke.

And even though she knew better, she silently begged him, *Please look at me like you did before, like you did last night when you were loving me. When I was loving you. Please look at me like you actually want me to be yours.*

Her silent pleas went unheard.

"Janica and I were just-" He cut himself off, that muscle in his jaw jumping. "We were just talking." He wouldn't meet Janica's eyes as he moved even further away. "I'll let you two catch up," Luke said, and then he was heading past Lily out the front door of the cabin as fast as his feet would take him.

And all Janica could do was watch him go.

Before she even realized Lily was there beside her, her sister's arms were around her.

Stupid tears threatened. Lily shouldn't even count as the "real" world. And yet, the second she'd walked in the door, Luke had separated himself from Janica as if she were carrying a contagious—and deadly—disease.

"It wasn't real," she said aloud. "Not for him."

Lily pulled back and brushed the hair out of her eyes. "Janica, honey, I know he just acted really weird, but I think I stunned both of you and—"

Janica pushed out of her sister's arms. "But nothing. It was fun. That's it."

Knowing better than to crowd her when she was like this, Lily stayed where she was as she said, "When I walked in, Jan, the way he was looking at you—" She paused, making sure Janica was listening to her before she continued. "In all the years I've known him, he's never looked at a woman like that, honey. Only you."

Janica couldn't respond, not with her throat clogged with emotion, not when she was bound to become a sniveling fool if she so much as opened her mouth.

Lily grabbed a bar stool and sat down on it, her expression one of deep consideration. "I can't believe how blind I've been this whole time."

"Oh come on. Everyone and their dog has been able to see how I felt about him."

"Not you, Jan. Luke. He's in love with you."

Wanting to believe it so bad it hurt, Janica shook her head, hard enough to make her eyeballs hurt.

"No. He isn't."

But Lily clearly wasn't listening, because she was saying, "You know what? I think he's been in love with you the whole time. Ever since Travis and I got together."

It was exactly what Janica had wanted to her. But she couldn't believe it.

Not anymore.

"He didn't even like me."

"No, honey, he loved you. And it must have scared the crap out of him. I can't believe I didn't see it. No wonder he always worked so hard to keep his distance from you. Because if he didn't, he knew you'd get in and make him admit his love for you."

As close to the verge of falling apart as she'd ever been in her entire life, Janica said, "I know you're trying to help. But please. Stop."

Because Lily was only making it worse by filling Janica's head and heart with hopes and dreams and wishes.

"Honey, I just know he's going to realize what he did, how stupid it was, and come back in that door any second now to tell you he loves you."

"Then you don't know your best friend very well," Janica said, not with anger, but with a sure knowledge that killed her.

But Lily was, in her own way, just as stubborn as Janica, so she tried another angle. "I've never known you to run from something you want. You love him, Janica. That has to be worth fighting for."

"I've been fighting with everything I have!" Janica half yelled at her sister. Forcing herself to calm down, she said, "I thought I could keep fighting, but I-" Her voice started to shake and she had to stop, take a couple of deep breaths. “I was wrong. He can't even be with me around you. Now I don't even know what I'm fighting for, anymore.”

“His love, Jan.”

A lone tear slipped down Janica's cheek. “But can't you see, even if I get what I want, even if I force him to stay with me, no one wins?” She shook her head. “Because that isn't real love.”

Janica took another deep breath. Steadied herself. “Sorry you had to come all the way out here to check on me.” She made herself push forward even though all she wanted to do was throw herself into Lily's arms and sob her heart out. “I'll come by your house soon. Spend some time with you and the kids, okay?”

She knew Lily wanted to say a thousand more things, wanted to ask a thousand questions, but Janica simply couldn't let her do that, so she turned and went into the bedroom to go collect the few things she'd brought with her.

And to change out of Luke's shirt.

She wouldn't take any part of him that he didn't want to give her. Not his clothes.

And definitely not his heart.

* * *

Lily found Luke out on the beach in front of the house.

“She's loved you for so long, Luke. You know that.”

That was the thing about Lily, Luke thought.

She looked so soft. So easy. But she was made of steel when she needed to be.

The exact opposite of her sister, who seemed to be all steel, but was really so soft and sweet at her core.

Knowing he was acting like a coward, he turned to face his friend and sister-by-marriage. "I should have had her call you. I should have known you'd be worried."

Lily gave him a small smile, shaking her head. "My favorite part of all of that is the part where you think you can actually make her do anything, Luke." And then, "How long have you been in love with her?"

He had to turn away from his friend again to stare out blankly at the rolling ocean at his feet.

Was that what this feeling was?

Love?

Fuck.

Could he really be falling in love with Janica? He never would have picked her if he'd had a choice.

Suddenly, he had to wonder, did he have a choice? And if not, what the hell was he going to do?

He knew he loved being with her, both in and out of bed. He knew that she made him feel happier, lighter. But he didn't know if that was enough.

If it could ever be enough.

When he didn't say anything, he felt Lily's hand on his arm. "Tell me what's wrong, Luke. I know she's my sister, and I dearly love both of you, but you can talk to me. I'm your best friend."

It was the strangest thing, but her words didn't sit right with him. Suddenly, it hit him why that was.

"No," he said slowly. "You're not."

Lily looked like he'd slapped her and he quickly reached for her hand. "I'm sorry. I can't seem to say or do anything right today. What I mean is that I know Travis is your best friend now. And that's exactly how it should be."

"But that doesn't mean that you and I—"

He cut her off with a quick brotherly kiss to her forehand. "I love you, Lily. You know that. But right now, you're not the person I need to be talking to." He looked up at the cabin. "And I have a feeling that if I don't get back up there right now, the woman I owe my explanations to is going to be gone before I get a chance to talk to her."

Chapter Twenty

Janica sat on the couch in the living room, her sketchpad on her thighs, her pencil in her hand. More than anything she wanted to bolt, wanted to hide. But she couldn't leave without saying goodbye, like a coward.

She couldn't leave without seeing Luke one more time.

She heard footsteps on the stairs and her heart started thumping in an out-of-control rhythm.

He was barely in the door when he said, "I'm sorry."

She swallowed. Licked her lips. Closed her notepad and started to stand up.

But before she could get to her feet, he was skidding to a stop in front of her on his knees. He put one large hands on her legs.

"Please, let me try."

The warmth of him burned all the way through her body. She couldn't refuse him anything. Not yet.

Not when she wanted everything so badly.

Unable to trust her voice, she nodded, and he said, "You asked me some questions a couple days ago. I want to answer them now. Or at least try.

I don't know if I know all of the answers yet, but this time we've spent together is helping me figure them out a little bit."

This opening up was everything she thought she'd wanted. So then why did she still feel like her heart was barely beating?

"I came to your apartment that night because I—"

His voice faltered and her heart ached for him. "You don't need to tell me, Luke."

"Don't let me off easy this time, Janica."

She felt her eyes widen as she took in his beautiful face. He was asking her to help him. And even though her heart was breaking, she would.

"I won't." She forced herself to level him with a don't-bullshit-me gaze. "So why? What happened?"

He ran one hand through his hair. "I almost killed somebody. A little girl."

She couldn't stop her swift intake of breath. But at the same time, she couldn't believe him either.

"What really happened?"

"I was exhausted."

"I know. I remember how wiped out you were."

"I should have gone home, but I stayed at the hospital instead. Because I didn't have any reason to go home." He reached out, stroked her cheek. "Because I didn't have anyone to go home to."

Her mouth crept up in a half-smile of

recognition. "I know how that is."

"My colleagues were trying to tell me to get some rest, to let them take over, but I wouldn't listen. And then when we were in the OR, I—"

She leaned over and put her hand over his mouth. "Everybody makes mistakes, Luke."

But, oh God, touching his mouth was such a bad idea. Because the only thing she could think to do next was cover it with her lips.

Taking away her hand, feeling it tremble as she put it back on her lap, she said, "Is she okay?"

"I called to check in and heard she's doing great. No thanks to me."

"Funny," she said, "I never pegged you for the self-pitying type."

His eyebrows went up. "Is that what I'm doing?"

"Maybe. I wasn't there with you in the hospital, but it sounds like you've already beaten yourself up pretty bad about it. And besides," she said with a grin that she didn't really feel, "it finally got you to my doorstep, didn't it?"

"It shouldn't have taken that, Janica."

But it had.

She drank in his chiseled features, his all-male scent. If she stayed another sixty seconds she'd be tasting his mouth, ripping off his clothes and pulling him down over her.

It was time for her to go.

Clearly sensing her thoughts, he gripped the skirt of her dress in his fist.

"You also asked me if I like being a doctor.

If I became one because of my mother. A week ago I would've told you I loved my job. Now I don't know anymore. But yes, she's the reason."

"Don't let what happened one night when you were tired change the color of your career for you. You still love it. I know you do. Just like I know that your mother would be so proud of you. So proud of what you do. And who you are."

"When she died," Luke said softly, his eyes going slightly unfocused as he faded back into memories, "Travis pretty much fell apart. I knew exactly what I needed to do. I had to keep it together for both of us. And any time he acted like a dick, I needed to be even nicer. Wherever he took a risk, I made sure to play it safe. So there'd always be one of us there to fall back on."

"Like me and Lily," Janica said softly. "Only in reverse."

"I guess so."

"You've never had a chance to let loose before, have you?"

"Not until you, sweetheart."

His sweetheart shot like an arrow straight through her heart.

He must've seen the pain in her face, because he was suddenly saying, "Sorry isn't good enough for the way I behaved in front of Lily."

"You don't have to apologize for being honest. For feeling what you feel." She moved her hands over his and squeezed them. "I'm really, really happy for you. I'm really glad that you're finally starting to work through everything."

"Please don't say but."

She had to.

"But you were right."

His eyes flared with something that looked a hell of a lot like fear.

"No, sweetheart, I wasn't."

"You were. You and me, we're not going to work."

She didn't want to be the one to say goodbye. But she would.

Because she loved him that much. And he deserved to be with someone he could love wholly, without reserve.

And then, maybe, in the future, if he missed her enough, he would come ba—

No.

It wasn't just the way he'd acted around Lily. The hard truth was that she had no future with Luke in the real world. Because even if a man like him who'd always walked the straight-and-narrow could fall in love with the woman she was now, she knew with utter certainty that he could never truly let himself love the wild girl she used to be too. And that was the only way it would work...her heart came as a package deal.

All or nothing.

Which was why letting him go did not mean he was going to come back around to her.

Ever.

* * *

LOVE ME ***by Bella Andre***

Luke couldn't remember the last time he'd felt pain this intense. And he couldn't remember the last time he'd been this scared. Terrified of all those empty spaces Janica was going to leave him with.

All his life he'd done what was fair, what was expected of him. All his life he'd put helping other people over helping himself.

Right now, he had to try to help himself.

"Do you remember what you said? About not being able to stop yourself from loving me? No matter what?"

Even as the words came, he knew they weren't fair. He shouldn't be using her words of love against her.

Especially when he hadn't even come close to giving them back to her yet.

"Of course I remember," she said gently, as if she knew how deeply her leaving was going to cut him and she wanted to try to soften the blow in any way she could. "I'm keeping that promise, Luke."

He watched a tear fall down her cheek and had to touch her, had to brush it away. She turned her face into his palm for a split second and he prayed, silently begged the universe to give her back to him.

Please don't let her leave me.

But then she was pushing off the couch. Moving away.

Away from him.

Taking all of her warmth and softness with her.

LOVE ME ***by Bella Andre***

"I love you, Luke. Enough to know that you don't belong with me." She picked up her bag. "I've got to go now."

"How can you leave when I think I'm falling in love with you?"

She went completely still, not moving at all, not even blinking. "If you ever know for sure, let me know."

She was halfway down the stairs when he said, when he begged, *"Stay."*

She'd said the same thing to him that first night.

Now she was the one leaving without a backward glance.

Chapter Twenty-one

Janica had never worked harder. It was amazing the things she could accomplish without a heart.

She finally had her collection accepted by the department store chain in Japan that she'd been wanting to get into for years. One of her hand-sewn, one-of-a-kind dresses had been selected for display at the Museum of Fashion in Paris. Teen Vogue had called about a half-page feature on up-and-coming designers.

She was getting everything she wanted for her career.

And she was miserable.

Not that anyone knew it, of course. Not even Lily. Mostly because Janica had gone out of her way to avoid her big sister. Actually, she'd gone out of her way to avoid everyone. She hadn't seen her friends, hadn't gone dancing, had barely left her studio for fourteen days and nights.

Tonight, however, she'd been unable to come up with a good enough excuse to miss a family barbecue.

"He isn't coming, Jan," Lily had told her on the phone that morning.

"It's okay if he does."

It wasn't, of course. Saying that was nothing but sheer bravado. But the thing was, even though it wasn't at all okay now, it was going to have to get okay.

Because at some point she was going to have to learn to deal with him.

At some point she was going to have to learn how to be in the same room with Luke and still be in love with him.

At some point she was going to have to figure out a way to watch Luke talk or drink or walk around and not replay, in excruciating detail, how it had felt when she was being touched by his hands, kissed by his mouth.

And at some point her brain was going to learn how to stop replaying his parting words.

I think I'm falling in love with you.

Obviously, though, he'd been wrong. Because she hadn't heard a word from him in the two weeks since she'd left the cabin in Big Sur.

After making a pit stop at the cupcake store, she headed over to Lily and Travis's house. The kids greeted her as if it had been a lifetime since they had seen her.

"They've missed you, Jan," Lily said. "We all have."

"Cupcakes."

She held the box out between them, as if she were trying to use it as a barrier, as a way to keep Lily from trying to get her to spill out everything she was barely holding back. But when Lily took the box and put it on the counter, judging by the way her sister was looking at her, Janica had a bad feeling about the barbecue.

"He's coming," Janica said in a flat voice.

Lily nodded. "I'm sorry. When Travis told me I could have killed him."

"There's nothing to be sorry about. Like I said before, I'll deal."

Not well, probably, but that was beside the point.

Violet reached a dirty hand into Janica's bag and pulled out some pretty pink ribbon and tulle. "Is this for me?"

"You bet," Janica said, picking up the bag and heading into the backyard. "We are going to make you and Sam some special barbecue outfits."

Lily spoke in the soothing tone that Janica remembered so well from their childhood. "He's going to come to his senses, honey. I know he is."

But Janica was already measuring ribbon and tulle.

* * *

Fourteen sunrises. Fourteen sunsets. Three meals a day. A handful of hours of sleep every night.

Every minute, every second, he'd missed her.

On the phone with Travis that morning, his brother had mentioned a barbeque. Evidently, Lily hadn't said a word to her husband about finding

Luke and Janica up at the cabin together. If she had, Luke knew he would have never heard the end of it from his twin.

Why, he'd wondered, had she kept something so big from her husband?

But it hadn't taken a brain surgeon to figure out why.

Lily was waiting for Luke to tell his brother—to tell the entire goddamned world—how he felt about Janica.

Hell, they were all waiting for that.

When he'd asked Travis if Janica was going to be there, his twin had said, "I think so. Lily said something about cupcakes. That usually means her sister is attached to them. I swear, she's a total sugar addict."

A flash of kissing her sweet lips, sticky from s'mores, on the beach had assaulted him.

The sound of Janica's laughter floated all the way out to the sidewalk and he stumbled, nearly dropping the bottle of wine he was holding. The front door was unlocked and he let himself inside. After putting the merlot down on the kitchen counter, he walked into the living room where there was a sliding glass door that led out to a huge atrium.

Janica was dancing with the kids to a pop song he'd often heard playing at the hospital. Violet and Sam were dressed in ribbons and fabric and Janica was holding their hands and spinning in a circle.

He swore to God he'd never seen anything

or anyone so beautiful in his entire life.

He loved her.

Nothing had ever been so perfectly, blatantly obvious.

All these years he'd tried to tell himself she was all about taking. But he'd been blindly, stupidly wrong about her.

She'd given and given to him, never once asking anything for herself. And looking at her with her niece and nephew, seeing, knowing how completely open and joyous she was with them, the truth hit him like a ton of bricks.

He'd lied to himself all those years—wasting each and every one of them—to try and keep himself safe. Safe from losing someone he loved again.

When it turned out that the only true safety he'd known since he was ten years old was with Janica.

It didn't make any sense. He wasn't at all sure how—or if—she would fit into his world, but none of that seemed to matter anymore. If the two of them had to go live on a remote island to make it work, that's what they'd do.

Travis came around the corner just then, clapping him on the shoulder. "Hey bro. Just in time for the grilling to begin."

That was when Janica looked up and finally saw him, her eyes going wide, her face flushing an even deeper shade of rose.

He didn't answer his brother. Instead, he walked straight over to the woman who meant everything to him. The woman who had given him her heart again and again.

"I—"

The part of him that still couldn't believe he was going to say it—to Janica of all people!—made him pause.

Damn it. What was wrong with him?

She needs to know how you feel. And then maybe, if you're the luckiest son of a bitch on the planet, she'll take you back. Just spit it out already. You might not have picked her, but that doesn't matter anymore. It wasn't your choice to love her, but that doesn't change the fact that you do.

It isn't going to kill you to say it, to admit the way you really feel. Maybe it will even save you.

"I love you."

The kids continued to dance around her as the song played on, but Janica just stood there and stared at him.

Why wasn't she throwing herself in his arms? Why wasn't she saying the words back to him.

"I love you," he said again. "I can't help myself. I've tried for so hard, for so long to stop feeling what I feel for you, but the truth is I've never been able to help myself, Janica. It shouldn't have taken me this long to figure out that I love you. So much, sweetheart."

The tension between them grew so palpable that even the kids stopped dancing. Lily, Travis, and both kids stood in silence, all of them waiting for what came next.

Finally, Janica dropped the children's hands and moved toward him. His heart had just started to beat again when she said, “Thank you for letting me know.”

And then, instead of walking into his arms, she walked past them.

All the way out the door.

And out of his life.

* * *

He heard Travis say, “Take the kids, Lily,” and then his brother was right there in his face.

“What the fuck was that?” His twin was incredulous.

“I love her.”

And he'd lost her.

Travis shook his head, looking more confused than he ever had. “I don't get it. You and Janica? How? When? Where?”

“A few weeks ago. I went to her apartment.”

He'd been in pain and she'd been the person he'd turned to. The only person who could give him what he must have known he desperately needed.

Not just her body.

But her heart too.

“She's right, you know. I don't deserve her.”

“Look, Luke. I don't know what the hell is going on with the two of you, but you've got to see that it could never have worked between the two of you. I mean, Janica is—”

He had his brother's shirt in his hands so

quickly neither of them saw it coming. “Janica is what?”

After thirty-five years of Travis playing the tough guy and Luke playing the nice guy, everything switched in an instant.

“Say it,” Luke dared his twin, wanting nothing more than to pound his brother's face into the pavement.

Clearly seeing the raw violence pounding through Luke's veins, Travis backed down. “I'm sorry, man. I like her. You know I do. I'm just surprised by your coming here and saying that to her.”

Luke forced himself to drop his brother's shirt. “Tell Lily I'm sorry I can't stay.”

Chapter Twenty-two

An hour later Travis walked into Janica's studio as if he owned the place. She purposefully ignored him. Which wasn't easy to do when he was hunkering over her, huge and angry.

"Hey sis. How's it going? Since you missed dinner, I brought you a burger."

She didn't buy the greeting. There was nothing easy, nothing nice about it apart from the actual words.

"I'm busy. What do you want?"

"We need to talk."

Still not bothering to look up from her computer where she was double-checking orders for the month, she said, "Fine. Talk."

"What the fuck kind of game are you playing with my brother?"

Knowing her own eyes were blazing now, she shot back, "You want me to draw you some dirty pictures?"

His mouth tightened, the mouth that was so like his twin's and, yet, so completely different. Of course she saw the surface similarities between Luke and Travis, but to her, that's all they were. Surface stuff.

LOVE ME *by Bella Andre*

She wasn't in love with Travis. She would never, ever be in love with Travis.

But she loved Luke with every goddamned cell of her body.

She watched Travis take a step back from her desk, walk to the window to look at the crowded city streets below.

"You know I've always thought you were a little bit crazy, right?"

He wasn't trying to be mean, and the truth was she didn't take offense. It was just the way she and Travis talked to each other.

"Yup," she agreed. "And you know I've always thought you were a little bit of an asshole, right?"

Finally, the hint of a grin.

"But here's the thing—I never thought you were stupid, Janica. You're one of the smartest people I've ever met. Both you and my brother have big, huge brains."

Her stupid heart skipped a beat at the mention of Luke, damn it.

"So then why the hell are you acting so stupid now?"

It killed her not to combat his awful words with worse words of her own. But, really, what was the point? Nothing Travis did or said was going to change the truth of the matter.

Luke didn't want to love her. And she couldn't do a damn thing to change that.

Except for stupidly, foolishly hoping that maybe, at some point in the future, he'd look at her and see everything he wasn't seeing now. Because didn't he see that loving her despite himself wasn't enough?

"I've got a lot of work to catch up on," she said by way of a get-the-hell-out.

But Travis didn't get the picture. Or, maybe he did, but he didn't give a fuck what she wanted him to do.

"We all know you're in love with him."

She met Luke's twin's gaze with clear, direct eyes.

"I am. So ridiculously, pathetically in love with your brother that I can hardly believe it." A muscle in Travis's jaw twitched in what she figured was shock and she continued with, "And trust me, he knows it."

After all, she'd only told him about a hundred times.

Clearly caught off guard by her sensationally straightforward admission, Travis stopped, stared, then sat down hard on her leather couch.

"Fuck."

It was, quite possibly, the biggest moment of solidarity she'd ever had with her sister's husband.

"I feel exactly the same way."

He shook his head, confusion taking over his face. "So then why won't you take him back?"

It was easiest to say, "Because I'm a bitch."

His eyes softened. Just slightly. "You're not a bitch."

"But it would be easier if you thought that

was the reason."

Not just for him, but for her too.

"You're right," Travis agreed. "It probably would be. But I'd rather hear the real reason."

She thought about it for a second. "I really don't want to have to say the words aloud to you, Travis."

He nodded and she thought that maybe, just maybe, he was going to go now and she would be left alone in her abject misery. Instead, he said, "All my life, until Lily came along, Luke was the most important person in the world to me. He was the only one who really knew me. Who saw through all my bullshit. But the thing is, I don't think I've ever been able to see all the way through his. I've seen him work himself into the ground, I've seen him date women who are so cold you wouldn't want to touch them with your tongue because it would stick. But I've never seen him like this, Janica. Help me help him."

They were more words than she'd ever heard strung together out of her brother-in-law's mouth. Now it was her turn to be stunned.

"What makes you think I know how to help him?"

"I can't believe I'm about to say this," he said, looking well and truly appalled, "but on the way over here I started to see things differently. Different enough that I actually think you're perfect for him. You're not one of those frigid bitches he's always been with. He knew he wouldn't fall in love with any of them. But you...well, clearly he didn't know what the fuck to do about you. Which is why I'm thinking that you might be the only person on the planet who can get through to him. The only person who can actually reach him." He shook his head. "I may need to go have my head examined after this."

"Good idea," she said, working like hell to fight back the rush of moisture that was building behind her eyeballs at her brother-in-law's unexpected words.

But his eyes saw too much, damn him.

Damn all the Carson men.

"You haven't told me yet why you won't take him back. Especially when I can see how badly you want to."

She couldn't sit behind her computer anymore. Her legs were itching to move, to run—and keep running. Away from everything that was hurting so bad. But even as she jumped up out of her chair, she realized not only did she have nowhere to go, but that even if she tried, she'd never be able to hide out, she'd never be able to steal away from her feelings.

"I just can't."

"Have you heard a word I've said?"

"And then some," she muttered. "Look, it doesn't matter what you think or what Lily thinks or even what I think."

She shook her head, hated the way she felt, like she was going to break apart, literally shatter from the inside out.

"It just doesn't matter."

"It does, Janica." He paused. "He told you he loves you. In front of all of us."

Her nostrils flared. She swallowed. Fought for whatever last shred of composure she retained.

"That was really big of him to do it like that. The grand gesture. You must have been really impressed."

"Fuck being impressed, Janica. The point is he did it. He said it. He feels it. So why the hell are we sitting here having this discussion? Why are you sitting here arguing with me instead of making his life a living hell?"

No.

This was where she had to draw the line. She wouldn't sit here and explain how it had felt to hear Luke say, "I love you," while everything else about him said he'd failed. While every piece of him clearly screamed that he couldn't believe he'd actually gone and fallen for the notorious, the slutty, the wild-child Janica Ellis.

"I want to be with—" She cut herself off and started over. "I need to be with someone who actually wants to love me." She felt the edges of her mouth start to wobble and sat back down behind her desk, putting her fingers on her keyboard in a desperate attempt to steady herself.

"Not just someone who can't help himself."

* * *

Lily lay in the curve of Travis's arms later that night. After putting the kids to sleep, he'd made the sweetest, most passionate love to her. Every touch, every kiss, every stroke of his body inside of hers had been pure emotion.

Pure love.

On the verge of falling into a deep, sated sleep, she heard him say, "You haven't asked me about my conversation with your sister yet."

She shifted out of his arms and sat up in the bed, moonlight streaming over her lush curves. "You didn't seem ready to talk about it yet."

His eyes drank her in, roving from her face to her breasts and stomach and hips, then back up to her eyes. "My God, sweetheart, you're so damned beautiful."

She reached for his hand and threaded her fingers through his, knowing she'd never get tired of hearing him say those words. Even though she saw the truth of it in his eyes every time he looked at her.

"I love you," she said, and then, "So what happened?"

"I was wrong about her."

Another time she might have laughed at his look of almost physical pain from his admission, but she couldn't. Not when she was so terribly worried about her sister. And his brother.

"She's not playing Luke," Travis said. "She really, truly cares about him." His face tightened even further. "He needs her in a way that he doesn't need you or me. And I'm afraid he's going to lose her."

Her heart was so heavy a couple of tears fell

before she even realized she was crying. "I'm afraid of that too."

"Hell," Travis said. "I'm thinking if things don't change soon, we're going to have to get them on a plane to Italy and force the issue."

Her eyes sparkled at the memory of their surprise wedding. "Oh, wouldn't it be amazing to see them up on that stage at the Festival of Weddings?"

Travis pulled her back into his arms and loved her tears away, but even after he fell asleep with his head on her chest, she couldn't stop worrying. Because she knew that dragging her sister and brother-in-law off to Italy wouldn't make a lick of difference.

She and Travis couldn't make the decision for them.

Luke and Janica needed to choose love for themselves.

All she could do was pray that they did. Because Luke and Janica meant everything to her.

And they both deserved the kind of forever love that she and Travis shared.

Chapter Twenty-three

As soon as Janica touched down in Italy, she knew she should get right back on the plane.

She always loved Italy. The architecture. The passionate natives. The food. The fashion. And as soon as Travis had left her office, she'd booked the next flight out to Milan to deal with some accounts that she'd recently picked up and to get a feel for the new fabrics and styles coming out of fashion's center of business.

But neither of those were the real reasons she'd gotten on the plane.

She'd had to leave. Had to get away from any and everything that reminded her of Luke.

Only, how could she have forgotten that she'd been here, in Italy with him, when they'd been trying to help Lily and Travis with their own roller-coaster relationship?

I love you, he'd said. *It shouldn't have taken me this long to figure it out.*

Okay, so he'd finally owned up to his feelings. But how long would it take him to accept them? To embrace them? To not be embarrassed by his feelings for her or to wish he didn't feel them? And if she had to tell him, if she had to give him step-by-step instructions on how to really and truly love her, then how could it possibly be real? And in the end, she couldn't force him to feel anything other than what he really, truly felt.

Only, it was one thing to try and resist Luke from 5,000 miles away. It was another entirely to think that she'd be able to do it when they were both back in San Francisco, meeting regularly at family events.

One touch, the slightest stroke of his fingers against her skin, and she knew she was going to be lost.

She'd loved him too deep, for too long.

Janica had never settled for anything her whole life. But if Luke could only love her part of the way, maybe settling for whatever he could give her was something she'd need to learn to live with.

Not even bothering to pick up her luggage, she stepped up to the ticket counter and got herself on the return flight out to San Francisco. A dozen hours later as she got off the airplane, knowing she couldn't go another second without seeing Luke, she told the taxi driver to take her straight to the hospital.

And then, from out of nowhere, she felt the truck in the lane beside them clip the back bumper, spinning the taxi off into the center divider on the freeway. Everything went black.

* * *

"Taxi crash. Twenty-nine-year-old woman.

Head wound. Possible internal bleeding."

Luke was heading into his tenth hour for the day and had just downed his fifth cup of coffee. He'd worked much longer hours in the past, but now the days seemed longer than they ever had. Coming off his four-week leave, he still felt tired, like he was dragging all the time.

And yet, at the same time, his hours in the ER were the only time he even felt remotely alive.

Somehow, none of the things that used to give him a rush, not even a car accident victim who would need every ounce of his concentration, set off a spark inside of him. Whereas Janica, with nothing more than a wicked little smile, had made him feel like it was the Fourth of July every single day.

Every single moment.

He was still amazed to realize that in less than a week she'd taught him how to have fun. How to appreciate everything around him. And how incredible it was to share his life with someone else.

How had he screwed everything up so badly? And how the hell could he possibly win her back?

The first time she said "I love you" he should have been right there with her, showering her with everything he'd felt for her for so long—and had so stupidly held back. He'd been scared to love and lose again. But he'd had no idea just how much it would really hurt. Especially when the losing part was entirely his fault.

Grabbing the chart from the paramedic, he moved to the quickly moving gurney and finally looked at his patient.

Oh God.

No.

Please, let this be a nightmare.

Please, God, please let this not be real.

But the blood across Janica's forehead and cheek, dried in clumps in her soft hair was real. Her pale skin, her closed, bruised eyelids were real. Her small body, so still and lifeless beneath the thin white sheet—so completely different from the way she normally was, the woman who didn't know how to stop moving—was real.

All of the patients he had ever worked on throughout his years in the ER came down to this moment.

The moment when he needed to save the woman who meant everything to him.

One of the first things he'd learned as a doctor had been that emotions had a time and place, but not in the operating room. He'd always known how to segment the surgeon from the flesh-and-blood man.

He called out instructions one after the other, held out his hands for the nurse to put on his gown and surgical gloves, while his brain worked methodically to assess the damage to Janica's body.

Sweetheart, please hold on. I'm going to save you. I promise.

But before he could lay even a finger on Janica, he felt a hand on his arm.

Luke looked at Robert, frowned as his colleague said, "You're crying."

Without thinking, Luke reached up to touch his face. He couldn't feel any wetness through the latex of his glove. And yet, he knew Robert was right about his tears.

Because no matter how hard he tried to push his emotions into the appropriate box, it just wasn't possible. Not this time.

Not with Janica up on the operating table.

"Do you know her?"

"She's the woman I love."

It was as easy as that.

They all watched him carefully, the operating room nurses, the doctor he'd worked with and socialized with for so many years. No one said anything. No one made the suggestion that he should step away. No one told him he wasn't equipped to do this job right now. No one tried to make him see that Janica would be better off in somebody else's hands.

Thank god, this time they didn't need to say it.

Walking away from the operating room with Janica on the table bleeding and hurting, trusting someone else to heal her and make her whole, was going to be the hardest thing he ever did.

But he had to do it.

For her.

"Please," he began, but Robert just shook his head, letting him know he didn't have to say anything more.

"We'll take good care of her, Luke. Don't you worry for even one second about that. You're going to have a long life with her. I promise you that."

Luke's feet felt like lead as he left the operating room. He couldn't go to the waiting room. But his legs wouldn't hold him either. Slowly, he slipped down against the wall until he was sitting on the floor. His head was in his hands and his heart, well, his heart was barely beating.

As the minutes slowly ticked down, he could feel himself alternating between numb and scared.

Scared shitless.

But although he had been crying in the operating room, he wasn't crying now. He didn't even have the relief of tears.

If anything happened to her, anything more than the crash, if something went wrong on the operating table, Luke knew he'd never feel anything again.

He simply couldn't live without her.

Somewhere in the back of his brain he knew he should call Lily, that she needed to know her sister was in the hospital, but he couldn't do it. Not until he knew more.

And all the while, the urge to bust into the OR and take over was so strong it took every ounce of control he possessed not to storm back in there and yank the instruments out of Robert's hands.

"Luke? What are you doing here? On the floor?"

He lifted his head, as heavy as a bowling bowl, and saw Dr. Jones, the woman who'd sent him off on leave, standing in front of him.

"Waiting."

He was surprised when she joined him on the floor. "Waiting for who?"

"Janica."

He didn't say anything more. He didn't say that she was his sister-in-law. He didn't say that he had been in love with her for so many years, there was no pinpointing the exact date or time when his feelings had become clear. He didn't tell her that Janica had offered to give him everything he'd ever wanted, even when he was giving her nearly nothing in return. He didn't tell her that he'd screwed everything up.

The psychiatrist's voice was gentler than he'd ever heard it. "I don't know what the situation is here, but you've got to know that she's going to be okay, Luke. Every doctor in the hospital is the best at what he or she does." When he didn't say anything, just let his head fall back to his knees, she squeezed his hand and said, "Let me know if you need anything. I'll be in my office."

Intellectually, Luke knew she was right. His colleagues were the best in the business. But deep inside, he wouldn't believe it until he heard Janica laugh again.

He wouldn't believe it until he saw her dance again.

He wouldn't believe it until he saw her twirl Violet and Sam, dressed in pink lace, around in Lily and Travis's living room.

Then, and only then, would he believe it.

And he'd never stop telling her he loved her.

He'd never stop trying to get her to see that she could love him back without fear. Because he'd never be so stupid again.

After what felt like hours, the operating room door opened. His colleagues walked out and were clearly surprised to find him on the floor.

For nearly two decades people in the waiting room had tried to read his face, post-operation. Now, he was the one looking for clues. For anything that would tell him if she was going to be all right. Or if she had—

"How is she?" The words came out harsh. Raw.

"She's young and healthy and things couldn't have gone better," Robert said with a reassuring smile.

They were the same words Luke had said to strangers a thousand times before, but this time, each one was his own nugget of gold. Relief hit him so hard that if he hadn't already been on the floor, that's exactly where he would've ended up.

"Thank you."

Those two whispered words held every ounce of his gratitude.

"Just like I told you," Robert said softly, "we wouldn't have let anything happen to her, Luke."

With Robert's help, Luke got up off the floor and followed Janica into the recovery room. Doctors didn't stay with patients, obviously. And usually, loved ones didn't either immediately postsurgery. Luke had never broken protocol like this before.

But nothing would stop him from breaking the rules this time.

He was not going to leave her side. And as he watched her sleep, needles in her arm, bandages on her head, her vital signs moving across the digital screen above her bed, he heard her voice in his head from that night out on the beach in front of the bonfire.

I knew I'd regret it forever if I didn't go for what I wanted.

She'd been so right.

And that was when another bomb hit him: He already knew he loved her.

But he hadn't realized until this very moment that she was his entire soul.

Chapter Twenty-four

Janica felt like crap.

Hangovers like this always made her want to roll over and go right back to sleep. Unfortunately, she knew from painful experience that she'd only end up feeling worse when she woke up again in a few hours unless she made herself get out of bed and take a couple of aspirin.

But when she tried to shift beneath the sheets, excruciating pain knocked the breath out of her.

"Don't move, sweetheart."

She immediately recognized Luke's voice. She would know it anywhere. Warm and sexy as hell. She tried to open her eyes, but they felt like she'd been walking through a sandstorm.

Fear hit her, then. What was wrong with her?

She tried to fight the pain, tried to surface all the way from her sleepiness. And then she felt his lips on her forehead, heard him softly say, "Shh," and his voice, his presence, was just what she needed to calm her down and lull her back to sleep.

* * *

"So thirsty."

She felt the rim of a plastic cup being held to her mouth and as she tried to gulp it down, she heard Luke say, "Not too much, sweetheart. Not yet."

She vividly remembered him saying nearly the exact thing when they were in bed together, when she was desperate to take all of him inside of her as fast as she could. But while she was presently in bed, they obviously weren't making love.

Everything hurt, especially her abdomen where it felt like someone had cut into her with a saw. Suddenly, it all came back to her, a series of flashbacks. The plane. The taxi. The truck hitting them. And then nothing but pain and darkness.

And a bone deep longing to be back in Luke's arms, safe and warm.

Her eyelids felt heavy, but she forced herself to open them anyway.

Just as she'd intended, she'd made it to Luke's hospital. Just not the way she'd planned to do it.

"I love you, sweetheart."

His sweet words had her shifting her somewhat blurry focus to Luke's face. Which was when she finally saw the tears streaking down his face.

"I love you," he said again, his voice thick with emotion.

And even in her fog, even as pain moved through her, she could see that everything was different.

LOVE ME ***by Bella Andre***

This love Luke spoke of wasn't the same kind of love that he'd felt before.

"I love you too," she said, but the act of speaking had her grimacing.

"Just breathe, sweetheart. I'm not going to leave you. I promise."

And even when a nurse came in and gave her more pain medication, Luke not only never let go of her hand the whole time...he didn't try to hide his tears.

Or his love for her.

She saw it, saw what she'd wanted more than anything, but even as the power of his love for her settled in, she suddenly realized that she couldn't believe it.

Now it was her turn to ask, "How can you?"

"How can I what, sweetheart?"

"How can you love me?"

She was surprised to see a small smile on his lips, his hand brushing a wisp of hair off of her forehead. "I love you because you're good."

She knew what he was doing. He was repeating all of the things she'd said to him back to her. But she knew it wasn't enough.

"You know I'm not good, Luke," she made herself say through the fog of pain, of exhaustion.

"Yes, you are."

"But I wasn't."

"I loved you even then." His eyes sparkled with something slightly wicked. "Even when you were bad. I wanted to be bad with you."

She didn't know what to say to that and in

her silence he hit her with, “I love you because you're honest.”

But even though she never lied, she had to say, “There are things you don't know about me. About my past. About what I've done. Things you won't like.”

Her words all came out in a rush and she only stopped when he put a finger to her lips. “I love who you are now. And I promise you, sweetheart, I love who you used to be too.”

“You couldn't.”

“I do, sweetheart. I love you for everything you do and everything you are. No exceptions. Past, present, and future.”

She'd never thought to hear him say this to her. Never dreamed he could accept her all the way through. And then she realized why that was.

“I never thought I'd find someone to love me for who I really am,” she said, tears streaming down her cheeks.

“You don't have any idea how loveable you are, do you?”

She shook her head and pain shot through her. But that was wasn't why she was wincing. It was because he was right. In her heart of hearts, she hadn't thought anyone could ever really love her. Because she hadn't truly loved – or accepted – herself.

“No,” she whispered.

“I love you because you're kind. I love you because you're sweet. I love the softness you keep hidden from everyone but me. I love you because you're the most loving person I've ever known."

He shifted his face so close to hers that his breath feathered across her lips.

"I love you because you're you."

And then, as he gently kissed her, Janica felt a true, deep warmth spread through her, starting deep in her heart.

Finally, amazingly, she'd found real love.

Chapter Twenty-five

Later, when she woke up in the dark, Luke was still holding her hand. His chair was pulled up to the side of her bed and his head was resting on the mattress in what had to be a distinctly uncomfortable position.

Even though she still felt like crap on the outside, on the inside, in the place where her heart had started to shrivel up and die, she felt great.

Amazing.

Fantastic.

Because she knew, without even a shadow of a doubt, just how much Luke loved her.

Sensing that she was awake, Luke lifted his head and smiled at her. He looked gorgeously rumpled, a world apart from the tightly wound doctor he'd been for so long.

Her love for him had been the last thing she'd thought of before everything went black after the crash.

"You saved me."

His smiled fell away, but he didn't let go of her hand. "No, I didn't. I didn't want anyone else to touch you, I didn't trust anyone else to save you, but I couldn't operate. Not when cutting into you would have been like slicing open my own heart."

Her insides warmed, her heart beating even stronger, steadier with every word he spoke.

"You stepped aside?"

"I'm sorry, Janica. I should have been stronger. I should have been the one—"

She didn't have the strength to throw her arms around him. Instead, she squeezed his hand and said, "Don't you see? You did save me. Because you made sure I got exactly what I needed." She paused as a tear slipped down her cheek. "You made sure I would be here to keep loving you, Luke. Forever."

* * *

He knew how weak she was, how tired, and yet he had to kiss her again. Gently, he pressed his lips to hers, only a little surprised when she kissed him right back much harder.

Janica Ellis was one tough chick.

His tough chick.

He wanted to believe her, wanted to believe he really had played a part in saving her.

"I can see your brain whirring into overdrive," Janica said. "Share with me. Please."

He looked at her, her big brown eyes so full of love. Understanding. He'd never given her his complete trust. He'd never shared all of himself with her. Because he'd been afraid.

But almost losing her had scared him more than anything else ever could.

Even letting her into the deepest darkest parts of his heart.

"When my mother died, everything changed."

"Of course it did."

"No." He didn't want her to let him off the hook this time. "I changed. I thought that maybe, somehow if I'd been a better son, a better person then maybe I could have saved her."

"You were ten years old."

"And I've spent the last twenty-five years trying to save her."

Tears were coming again now, not just from Janica, but from him too. He never cried, hadn't cried one single time since he was ten years old.

Not until last night.

"It's time for me to let go." He ran his thumb across the top of Janica's hand. "I know that now. Because of you. I need you so badly. I've always needed you."

He wasn't surprised by her smile, even as tears ran from her eyes. "I know that. I've always known it." Her smile wobbled. "I need you too."

But that was still what he didn't understand. "Why me? You're beautiful, incredible, brilliant. You could have anyone."

"I kept telling myself to stop loving you. To stop being stupid and praying for you to come around, but I couldn't help it. You're it for me, Dr. Carson. The only man I'll ever want again. The man I want to have children with and share my future with. I want you to be the husband I can count on and I want nights of incredible passion with you and I want you to be my best friend. I even love all of the things I tease you about."

Working like hell to take everything she was saying in and knowing he was failing, that he was going to have to ask her to say it all again and again, he said, "And you taught me how to have fun. You showed me everything I've been missing, everything I've been blind about. I don't want to be blind anymore."

"Don't worry," she said with that wicked grin he couldn't help but love. "I'm always going to make you try wild things. And I'm always going to drive you crazy." But then, her grin shifted to something far less joyful. "But I'll try not to embarrass you too much in public. And here at work."

Something shifted in him, again, that awful realization about what she'd said regarding Travis that night out on the beach. *I see the way he treats Lily. I know how good he is to her. But that doesn't change his past.*

Her past. Even after all the reasons he given her about why he loved her, she was worried about the things she'd done. Worried that he would use them against her.

"I know who you were, Janica. And I know who you are now. I love every part of you. The old. The new. Everything you're going to be. I will never be embarrassed by any part of you. You're not going to make me spank you for not listening, are you?"

She blinked at him, a myriad of emotions

crossing her face. “No. I won't make you spank me. Not for that anyway.”

His cock stirred even as he tried to stay on task. “I am going to keep loving you every single second for the rest of your life. When we're laughing. When we're making love.” He paused, grinned. “Even when we're fighting and I have to turn you over my knee and bring my palm down on your sweet little ass to make my point.”

She grinned. “We are going to fight, aren't we?”

“And then we're going to make up.”

Her wicked smile came back, bigger, more full of sensual promise than ever before. “Oh yes, we are.”

LOVE ME *by Bella Andre*

Chapter Twenty-six

Two months later at the Festivale di Matrimonio (The Festival of Weddings) in Saturnia, Italy....

"I can't believe we're back," Lily said as she hugged Janica tightly.

Janica could hardly believe it herself. The Tuscan village was as beautiful as she remembered. Music was playing on every corner, people were dancing in the street. Lily laughed when Travis came to steal her away and twirl her around in his arms as the sun began to set behind the ancient buildings.

Luke came out of their hotel then, and stole her breath away as he looked at her with those dark, dangerous eyes.

"I love you."

She lifted her mouth to his and kissed him with all the emotion in her heart.

"Will you marry me?" he asked against her lips.

"How about we do it tonight?" she whispered back, loving his laughter.

LOVE ME ***by Bella Andre***

* * *

Italian women in wedding gowns walked hand-in-hand with Italian men in their finest suits. Lanterns blinked colorful lights along every narrow street. Bells rang out from the church tower as children splashed in fountains.

A middle-aged woman reached for Janica's hands and with a final loving look at Luke, she let herself be led away to a tent full of women.

One of them held a beautiful, old-fashioned wedding dress and tears sprang to Janica's eyes. She would have never designed a dress like this for herself.

But it was perfect.

Soft hands removed her dress, then slipped the wedding dress on over her head. Other hands brushed her hair, added makeup, sparkly glass jewelry. At the end, they covered her hair and face with a thin lace veil.

When they were finished, there was a loud whistle and the band began to play again. While everyone clapped in time to the music, Janica walked into the piazza. She looked up at the stage, saw Luke waiting for her there with the priest, and nearly stumbled on the cobblestones.

He had on a traditional bright red, orange, and yellow striped sash around his waist and he'd never looked more beautiful than he did right then, on the verge of declaring his love for her in front of an entire town.

She'd been in love with him for so long that

she could hardly believe this was real.

But it was. Wonderfully, amazingly real.

She saw Lily holding Travis's hand off to the side of the stage, but before Janica could make it all the way to Luke, Lily came down toward her.

"Luke is the only person I could ever give you up to. I love you so much, baby sister."

"I love you too, big sis."

Lily held her hand all the way up the steps. And then Janica's hand was in Luke's, and the priest began speaking, the language lyrical and beautiful and mysterious. When he was done, he handed her a thin green vase.

She vividly remembered Lily and Travis's wedding here on this very stage and knew what she and Luke were supposed to do. Judging by the laughter in his eyes, she knew he remembered too.

"I'll bet you've been dying to smash this vase for five years, haven't you?" he asked softly.

She laughed and reached for him, but he was faster than she was, and instead of throwing the vase down, when he kissed her and she forgot everything but him, everything but how much she loved him, everything but how good it was to be loved right back, the vase slipped from her fingers.

And shattered at their feet.

Cheering broke out, loud, happy, and then she and Luke were being lifted off the stage while bright confetti seemed to fall straight out of the sky.

* * *

LOVE ME *by Bella Andre*

Luke carried Janica up the winding staircase to their hotel suite. Her eyes were closed and she snuggled against his chest.

"How are you feeling?"

It had only been two months since the car crash and he'd had serious reservations about Janica overdoing it on their trip.

"Good." She snuggled in tighter, her breasts rubbing provocatively against his chest. "Horny."

He almost stumbled on the final step. Had he heard her wrong? She hadn't opened her eyes, wasn't giving him that wicked little smile that he knew—and loved—so well. She had to be tired, didn't she?

But with one word, his cock had gone from half-mast to practically bursting.

He carried her into the bedroom and moved to lay her down on the bed. Her arms tightened on his neck.

"Stay."

God, he wanted to stay with her, wanted to take her, wanted to be inside of her more than he wanted to take his next breath. But two months ago she'd almost died. He didn't want to hurt her.

"It's been a big day."

Anger flared in her beautiful eyes. "I am sick to death of being treated like porcelain."

His own anger flared. "Damn you, we haven't even been married one night and you're talking back to me."

At his response, her eyes flared again, but not with anger this time. With lust.

"Then I guess you'd better find a way to shut me up," she challenged.

His cock throbbed in his tuxedo pants and he knew what she wanted. What they both needed.

"Get on your knees, wife."

She immediately complied, a sinfully beautiful bride in her wedding gown, kneeling in front of the groom. Waiting for his next command.

"Show me how much you love me. Now."

Her long, slim fingers went to his zipper and the diamond on her wedding ring glinted in the light as she pulled it down.

And then, he was inside her mouth, his new wife's sinfully hot lips surrounding his throbbing cock. She licked and sucked at his arousal and he loved her so much he knew he wouldn't be able to hold on. Not tonight.

A second later, she was flat on her back and he was driving into her, hard, fast, deep.

"Love me, Luke," she whispered.

And he did.

* * *

He cradled her into his body, feeling safe and complete. "I was too rough."

"I love it," she whispered sleepily. "You've always known exactly what my body needs." She didn't say anything for several moments and he thought she was asleep. Until she said, so softly that he almost missed it, "My heart too."

And as he fell asleep, his new wife warm

and soft in his arms, it was exactly the same for him.

Janica knew him better than anyone ever had. Especially what his heart needed.

Her.

Forever.

THE END

LOVE ME ***by Bella Andre***

Get ready to find out how it all began in TAKE ME, Lily and Travis's incredibly passionate love story.

TAKE ME by Bella Andre

An appetite for sensual pleasures must never be denied. . . .

Lily Ellis has curves--soft, beautiful curves. The kind of voluptuous body she fears Travis Carson, the man she's always loved from afar, would never crave. But Lily is about to be proven wrong. Her sensual adventure begins when, despite her inhibitions, the demure San Francisco interior decorator agrees to model a plus-size dress for her fashion designer sister. Watching this sensual beauty move down the runway with mesmerizing power, Travis can't believe it's the same Lily he's always known and always rejected.

In a whirlwind of electric attraction, Lily is soon moaning Travis's name in his bed, not just in her wild fantasies. But Lily is all too aware that she's nothing like his past lovers . . and now that she has him close at last, she's praying Travis likes what he sees and feels. Determined to beat Travis at his own game by guarding her true feelings of love and lust, she spontaneously partners with him on a business deal that takes them all the way to Italy.

In the seductive warmth of the Tuscan sun, Lily is

about to unwrap her real self, and play a game of desire with the hot-blooded Travis. Will she be burned by an ecstasy that's so all-consuming it has her seeing stars? Or will Travis open his heart to the sexy, exciting, and lasting love she has to offer?

REVIEWS for TAKE ME....

"Oh, my! Bella Andre's TAKE ME is wonderfully sexy--a big, fun fantasy with an euqally big heart. You'll cheer these characters on as they find each other...and themselves!" ~Emma Holly, bestselling author

"TAKE ME is emotionally charged and deliciously erotic. A must-read from cover to cover." ~Jaid Black, bestselling author

"A story with a woman who isn't model perfect is a refreshing change in TAKE ME...Ms. Andre captures the beauty of Italy in such a way that it will leave one wishing to experience the warmth of the Tuscan sun..." ~ Patricia Green, Romance Reviews Today

"The sex scenes are hotter than a whole pot of five alarm chili and left me gasping for air. The plotline is intriguing and kept my eyes riveted to the pages. I loved this book! Take Me is a terrific book that I absolutely adored." ~Susan White, JustEroticRomanceReviews

LOVE ME ***by Bella Andre***

"You like it hot? Get yourself a copy of Bella Andre's Take Me. Her writing is hotter and sexier than ever. With fun dialogues, a breathtaking European setting and sympathetic characters, it's easy to be seduced by this story." ~Kris Alice, A Romance Review

"Packed with sizzle, but also contains a good balance of emotional pull. I found myself saddened when the journey ended." ~Tracy Farnsworth, Round Table Reviews

"TAKE ME is an excellent book about a full figured woman who like most has a complex about her weight. Bella Andre hasdone an outstanding job creating a heroine who is not average and a hero who loves her just the way she is." ~Angel, Romance Junkies

"I am lucky enough to work at a bookstore that received an advanced reading copy of Take Me. I was unable to put the book down. IT IS WONDERFUL!!!! And I will be recommending it to customers, friends, and family." ~ Tewanda Hardy, bookseller

LOVE ME *by Bella Andre*

AUTHOR BIOGRAPHY

Bella Andre has always been a writer. Songs came first, and then non-fiction books, but as soon as she started her first romance novel, she knew she'd found her perfect career. Since selling her first book in 2003, she's written thirteen "sensual, empowered stories enveloped in heady romance" (Publisher's Weekly) about sizzling alpha heroes and the strong women they'll love forever. If not behind her computer, you can find her reading, hiking, knitting, or lunching with her favorite romance writing ladies.

Bella lives with her fabulous husband and children in both Northern California and a ninety-year-old lakefront log cabin in New York's Adirondacks.

Please visit her on the web at www.BellaAndre.com

LOVE ME ***by Bella Andre***

Other titles by Bella Andre...

ECSTASY

Candace, a newcomer to writing erotica, is thrilled when Charlie, a veteran of the industry, agrees to be her mentor. But neither of them ever expected that Charlie's lessons on new positions, using toys, varying locations and role playing would spiral from verbal instruction into hot, hands on education. Unfortunately, Candace's deception about the new erotic romance she's writing--where Charlie plays the starring role--is about to threaten their one chance at true love.

Reviews...
4 1/2 stars from Romantic Times Magazine!!!
Andre writes a wonderful story filled with lovable characters and steamy sex. When Charlie agrees to mentor Candace, their lessons quickly become the hands-on variety, and they find that more than just a physical chemistry exists between them. Anyone looking for a funny and intelligently written read should definitely give this book a try!
~ Reviewed By: Derenda Hilbert, RT

"4 1/2 HEARTS! This book is wonderful and so hot it will melt your screen."
~ Reviewed by Lisa Wine for The Romance Studio

"The sparks fly when two erotica authors come together. The tension between Candy and Charlie is

electrifying. I really enjoyed getting to read snippets of Candy's novel as she wrote it. ECSTASY is truly that -- two authors discovering what real love is for the first time. It is a real winner. Don't miss it!"
~ Reviewed by Denise Powers, Sensual Romances

SHOOTING STARS

San Francisco, present: A bold and sensual woman, Christina wishes the men she took to bed could be more like the warriors of the past: strong, sexy and just a little bit scary.

Scotland, 1320: On the verge of marrying a great warrior, convent-raised Christiania prays for a gentle man to save her from marriage to a man she fears.

A shooting star and a fervent wish for their heart's desire are all it takes for both women's dreams and wildest sexual desires to come true…

Reviews...
"SHOOTING STARS is one of the greatest time travel romances that I have read. The characters are highly sensual and in touch with their sexuality. The storyline is sweet and romantic and the sex scenes are steamy. What more could you ask for? Ms. Andre pens an out of this world novella that makes you want to wish on shooting stars and believe in true love, no matter what the cost…

LOVE ME ***by Bella Andre***

~ Reviewed by Ansley Velarde for The Road to Romance

"Sassy and erotic, Shooting Stars is a great time travel. Both Christina and Christiania knew what they wanted and once they had it weren't afraid to grab it and do whatever necessary to ensure they kept it. Ms. Andre adds a high level of suspense and tension in addition to the love and sensuality. This is one you don't want to miss!
~ Reviewed by Sharon McGinty for In the Library Reviews

Made in the USA
Charleston, SC
30 August 2010